THE SECRET OF LIGHTHOUSE POINTE

A NOVEL OF GOTHIC ROMANTIC SUSPENSE

PATTY G. HENDERSON

THE SECRET OF LIGHTHOUSE POINTE

A NOVEL OF GOTHIC ROMANTIC SUSPENSE

PATTY G. HENDERSON

Published 2011

The Secret of Lighthouse Pointe
© Copyright 2011 Patty G. Henderson

A Black Car Publishing Edition
www.blackcarpublishing.yolasite.com

Cover Collage and Design: Boulevard Photografica
Interior Book Design: Boulevard Photografica
Editor: Claudia McCants

Visit the author site: www.pattyghenderson.com

This book is for my Mama, who passed into the loving arms of Our Lord on October 5th, 2010. I miss her more than I can put onto mere paper. I love you, Mama.

Acknowledgements

I finished this book during the pain and loss of losing my Mama, who passed away last year. I kept writing, hoping and praying that by consoling myself in writing, I could keep the heartbreak away. It was tough. There were times I thought the book worthless and thought of trashing it. But as time wrapped its arms around my hurt, I was able to realize that my Mama would have wanted me to finish my work.

I did and you're holding it in your hands.....or in your Kindle, Sony, Nook or other favorite eBook reading device. I couldn't have finished the book without the help of some wonderful friends. Terry Baker, your unfailing support and friendship have been a lifesaver in turbulent times. Thank you.

Claudia, this book would not have glimmered were it not for your help in the editing. You are the hand that buffed my rough draft into a glowing gem.

Patty G. Henderson
May, 2011

THE ARRIVAL OF CONSTANCE

CHAPTER 1

She was at the end of her rope and the only thing in the cabinet was poison. Constance Beechum held the letter of dismissal from the milliner in one hand and the half-filled bottle of sleep draught in the other. The coppery-colored liquid offered the end of her misery. An end to a life of poverty and endless disappointment. There would be no one to miss her and few to mourn her.

She gripped the stained bottle with the faded label tightly in her hand. There was nothing brave about taking one's own life. It was a total act of cowardice. But in her cold, totally lucid mind, it was merely an act of desperation.

Constance's morbid thoughts were interrupted by the clatter of heavy hoof beats crunching on the snow outside the lower end Boston boarding house she had been living in for the last year. She was certain she'd be out in the street come the weekend. She wouldn't be able to avoid Mrs. Tanner, the owner, for much longer. She'd already been kind enough to allow Constance a respite in her board rent for the last week.

She was only mildly interested in the loud footsteps echoing outside in the hallway. She never expected visitors. But there was definitely someone knocking on her door now.

1

Strong knocks. Surprised and somewhat concerned, Constance wondered if she should open the door or just ignore who might be on the other side. Would Mr. Pennock, the corner grocer, come demanding his due for the oatmeal she'd gotten with an IOU?

"Miss Beechum? Is there someone there?" It was a man's voice, but not Mr. Pennock's. More knocking. "Miss Beechum, I've come at the behest of your uncle, the honorable barrister Mr. William Merriweather."

Constance put down the bottle of poison absentmindedly, springing to the door at the mention of her uncle's name. Standing outside her door was a large, older gentleman, surprisingly still wearing a short, white wig, carriage hat and light coat. He sported a trim, grey moustache. Under his arm was a slim, leather pouch.

"Miss Constance Beechum, I am to presume?"

"I haven't heard from my uncle in years." Last she'd heard, he was living in New York. She held the door open for him. "Please, come in, Sir." Her boarding room was barely the size of a large living room. The bed lay unmade beside the single window and her only dress draped lazily across the chair that sat facing a messy desk. "I must apologize. I never receive gentlemen here." She eyed her tiny living space.

"I won't stay long, Miss. My name is Richard Ware. I'm Barrister Merriweather's assistant. I've been sent only to make certain I can hand this letter to you personally and that the recipient is indeed Miss Constance Beechum."

Constance wondered how important the letter in the leather pouch could possibly be if her uncle sent his own assistant to deliver it to her.

"I am indeed Constance Beechum."

The man pulled out two pieces of paper, one folded over, and the other flat. "Allow me, Miss, to ask you to sign your name as proof of delivery." He handed her a short note basically verifying that Constance Beechum received the letter and that it was handed to her in person.

2

She left Richard Ware standing in the middle of the room and took it to her small table. Clearing off pewter cups and plates with leftover crumbs of bread, she signed the letter and took it back to the waiting man.

"I wish I could have seen Uncle Merriweather." She smiled, recalling wistfully the times of grand parties on the expansive lawns of Belvedere Park when she was only a child. The images of all the ladies with elegant dresses and hats and sailboats in the lake were forever part of her memories.

Richard Ware said nothing, only harrumphed, stuffed the signed form back in the leather pouch and tipped his hat. "Thank you, Miss. I'll be on my way."

He'd been uneasy in her tiny, broken down and cheap room. Constance could see it in the way he furtively eyed what little furnishings there were. Once he was gone, she sat down on her bed and opened the letter from her uncle. It was dated the twenty-fourth day of January, eighteen twelve.

My Dear Constance,

I regret that I've not been more mindful of you these years. You have been quite difficult to track down. It is unfortunate that I must find you in such dire need and circumstances. Why did you not seek me out for assistance? An unmarried young woman has very little recourse left but to either find a husband or suitable, long term employment.

It has come to my attention that you have neither. It is because of this that I have found you the perfect opportunity for stability and monetary relief.

I've been approached by the Gerard family of the fine city of Castine, Maine, for aide in finding suitable nursing care for the Lady Elizabeth Gerard. They have a fine estate, Gerard House, where you will live until Lady Gerard passes. I do not know if you have experience in these matters, but it will behoove you to mention nothing to the contrary if you wish to be accepted for the job. I have provided travel plans and coach for your journey and have been in correspondence with the Gerard family regarding your arrival. They are arranging for your transfer from Castine to their estate. Please follow the instructions I've outlined below, including the date of your departure and travel itinerary. I've also made arrangements at Presley's for any clothes or other feminine accessories you may need for your travels and stay.

If you should need to reach me after your arrival at Gerard House, please do so at the address above. Either I or my assistant, Mr. Ware, will handle your correspondence.

Sincerely,
William Merriweather

That was it? Fury with a tinge of sadness spread through Constance's insides like spilled ink. How could her uncle be so cold? She was being shipped off to some forsaken house in the middle of nowhere because her uncle had somehow found out she was living in squalor, unmarried and worthless? Well, maybe "worthless" was her own expression, but she certainly felt that way. How did he find out where she was and that she was without employment? Had Mrs. Hanley at the milliner shop written her uncle? Constance had given him as a reference. So, her uncle, absent all these years from her life, now expected her to just pick up all her things and take off to live with strangers? She tried to quiet her anger. On the other hand, the only other thing that awaited her here was the bottle of draught.

She glanced at the detailed instructions below her uncle's handwriting. She couldn't believe her eyes. The date she was expected to be at the coach depot was February 12th! That was two days from today! How could her uncle expect her to just drop everything, pack and run to jump on a coach to who knew where?

Constance lay back on her bed, sadness creeping up her insides like a slivering snake. Why not go? There was very little to pack and no one to miss her if she left. Not even Lily. No, the only people who were sure to come looking after her were her debtors.

Shoving away her thoughts of Lily and her nagging fears of what might await her at Gerard House, Constance got up from the bed, dragged her two small, tattered suitcases from underneath and began to pack. She only wished she didn't have so many unstitched holes in her gloves. It had been snowing on and off for days. It was going to be a cold trip to Maine.

Perhaps a shopping day at Presley's, one of the most exclusive establishments in Boston, would chase her gloom away.

CHAPTER 2

Light snow flurries had started up again. After a heavy snow fall, the sky was still an angry grey and swollen with the threat of more white flakes. The wind coming in from the Atlantic was icy and hit the skin like piercing needles. It was not an environment for man or beast.

Constance Beechum couldn't help but feel sorry for the driver of the coach, who seated outside, was at the mercy of the unforgiving elements. She sat alone in the small compartment of the enclosed carriage. It was probably a good thing, since the ride was so rough and bumpy, she feared she'd be seated atop the lap of the unfortunate passenger beside her. Not that she blamed the driver for the brutal ride. Roads were intolerable even in the most ideal situations. Add a blizzard and you've got a trip only a desperate woman, such as herself, would consider.

Constance sat with her back to the front of the coach, feeling more comfortable being closer to the only other person on the trip with her, the driver. The small panel just above her head slid back and the shrieking wind swept into the cabin.

He shouted, "We'll be coming upon the crossroads up ahead, Ma'am! Hard to tell in this snow, but the marker should be up soon!" She barely heard him over the intense wind. He slammed the panel shut again. Constance heard the snap of the whip on the horses. It sounded like gun shots.

Constance Beechum bundled deeper into her threadbare coat and cast her gaze out the window, content again to watch the fall of the snow, her grey eyes mirroring the color of the sky. Since leaving the warmth and comfort of the inn in New Hampshire, where she'd disembarked from the steamer and lodged for the night, the roads and landscape had grown bleaker and more desolate.

Every now and then, their path would wind through a cluster of small homes, but the brutal winter snowstorms kept most people shuttered inside. They traveled close to the coast. Before the snowfall made it nearly impossible to see beyond a few feet, she had glimpsed the heaving, ominous waters of the Atlantic as they broke with a thunderous roar against the mighty cliffs, spraying white and foamy.

Constance turned up the collar of her coat even higher around her thin neck. She was a fine looking woman, even as she approached the threshold of spinsterhood. Her high cheekbones, smooth white skin and naturally rosy cheeks garnered her no shortage of eligible young men. They came calling with flowers, candies and fine scarves. In Boston, and in the unblinking eye of society, declining their advances had become burdensome and the subject of too much talk.

And then there had been Lily.

Her thoughts were abruptly interrupted when she heard the driver issue a harsh order for the horses to pull up and the carriage began to slow down. The sound of the wind intensified and the carriage trembled in its fury. The panel behind her slid open and the driver's face peered down at her. His face was peppered from sheets of snow.

"Sorry, Miss, but there is a gentleman flagging the coach at the crossroads stop. We'll be a minute." He snapped the panel shut again.

Constance shivered but not from the cold. She wondered how safe it was to pick up passengers at a crossroads. She always assumed coach lines had passengers board and disembark at inns or coach stations. And who would be sane enough to wait at a crossroads marker in this kind of snow storm? She was sorry she hadn't asked the driver about that.

She heard only muffled conversation and then the carriage door opened in a whoosh of snow and wind and a man in dark coat and hat stepped inside, taking the seat across from her. He was covered in a sprinkling of snowflakes.

The carriage driver slammed the door shut without uttering a word. The new passenger was bundled in a heavy, black greatcoat that reminded Constance of a military-issued coat, with his collar turned up high, and his head topped with a large carriage hat. Its brim was much wider than was stylish and dropped down over his face, nearly hiding the gentleman's green, almond-shaped eyes. He wore thick gloves and a light grey scarf.

Even with the heavy outer garments, the man seemed thin and narrow. The only thing Constance could see fully of him was a slightly delicate square and clean looking jaw.

Saying nothing, he merely tipped his hat, nodded to her, and rubbed his gloved hands together briskly. Outside, the crack of the whip snapped again and the carriage jerked into motion again.

Her new companion removed his gloves, dusting the snowflakes on the floor lightly, and placed the wet gloves on the seat beside him. He leaned back, slipped his slouch hat even lower over his eyes, and set his gaze on Constance. The way he moved reminded her of some of the young men in the popular social circles of Boston. They were dandies, effeminate and concerned primarily with their looks and the latest fashions.

She fidgeted under his stare, bothered by his silence and his impertinent glaring.

8

"If I may be so bold, madam, to inquire why a lady would choose such an unGodly way to travel and in the middle of this Nor'easter?"

Constance was a bit miffed at the stranger's boldness, but his delicate voice both intrigued her and also confirmed her suspicions. She was certain that under the masculine-styled coat, lay a dandy for sure.

"I'd venture to respond, Sir, that the weather is as unGodly for you as it is for me." She faked a smile.

The man tipped his hat and smiled, revealing small and even teeth. "My pardon, Madam. I have been so ungentlemanly for not introducing myself." He leaned forward and took Constance's hand. "Most call me Mr. Kane."

"Everyone calls me Miss Beechum." Constance felt no threat. She couldn't help but notice how narrow and small-boned his hand was, but with a strong grasp. She caught the gleam of a small, square black ring on his index finger.

He sat back and continued to study her. "How far have you traveled, Miss Beechum, and where be your destination?"

Should she give out that much information to a total stranger?

"I've come from Boston. I'll be stopping off at Castine."

"Boston to Castine? My dear Miss Beechum, I'm aghast at the route you've chosen. Why did you not take a coaster up the coast?"

Why was she indulging this Mr. Kane? "My uncle advised against going by sea. The talk of a blockade or war with the British is heavy on his mind. He arranged my travel as he thought best and frankly, I'm very grateful for him doing so."

It was true. Her Uncle Merriweather feared the talk and very real threat of American and British hostilities. The war for independence from King George and his rule had barely ended and here they were in 1812 talking of battle again. President Madison threatened to blockade British trade ships from the lumber-rich colonial eastern states. They needed

American lumber to build their fleet of battleships. Her uncle had just played it safe for her sake.

"Well, your uncle is very wise. The drums of war are beating at a fierce pace, I'm afraid. Do you travel to Castine for your uncle, then?"

Constance smiled. Mr. Kane was as curious as a young lady in a social salon. "Oh, dear, no. I'm to be employed by the Gerard family at Gerard House."

"Gerard House?" Mr. Kane's voice raised an octave and he stiffened at her response.

"Yes, I'll be nursing and caring for the Lady Elizabeth Gerard."

Mr. Kane only nodded and remained silent.

Constance was tired of the personal questions. "So, Mr. Kane, do you think it true, then? Will the British and American ships get into it?"

"Yes, Miss, I believe they will."

The carriage, bouncing relatively little, began to slow then stopped. Outside, the snow persisted in a light drift. The driver pulled open the door and a big whoosh of icy air blew into the cabin.

"We've arrived at The Red Hen Inn and Tavern, Ma'am."

Kane quickly put his gloves back on, jumped out of the carriage before Constance and offered her a hand. She took hold of it and stepped out, slipping deep into a cushion of snow. The coach driver had already unstrapped her luggage from atop the carriage.

"Miss Beechum, may I ask one final question? Will you be expecting transportation to Gerard House?" He looked around at the absence of any coach or carriage at the inn. "I'd be honored to stay with you until your driver arrives."

Constance couldn't help but smile. Why were the dandies always attracted to her? "And will that not detain your travels? What coach shall you take then?"

He studied the falling snow and the heavy cover of it on the ground. Constance's smile widened. "Don't worry, Mr.

Kane, I will be quite alright. My uncle was assured that someone from Gerard House would fetch me."

Kane tipped his wide-brimmed hat one more time, reached for her gloved hand and pressed his full lips gently. "Be safe, Miss Beechum, and congratulations on your employ." He jumped back into the carriage and disappeared inside. The driver slammed the door shut and Constance watched as the driver snapped the whip. The horses lurched forward, and the carriage disappeared into the curtain of snow.

A strong gust of wind reminded her that The Red Hen Inn looked much more inviting than standing in the freezing snow.

The Inn was dark inside, but with drafts of welcoming warmth coming from a large fireplace of rough-hewn stones at the far end of the small room that appeared to be the tavern. It was a small establishment. There were only a handful of small, weathered wooden tables, several with chairs but others just benches. Several men huddled at a table in the back, a woman with a plain grey woolen dress and white apron, was busy setting pewter mugs on the table, her mop cap slightly askew on her head.

The scent of apples baking mingled with a dash of stale ale. A rather large and round man wearing black pantaloons, black shoes, a white shirt with dark vest and white apron, approached her. His head of thinning, white hair was bare and he wiped his hands on his apron as he beamed at her.

"Good day to you, Ma'am."

"Miss Beechum, Sir." Constance smiled back.

"Mighty big snow storm, Miss Beechum. Welcome to the Red Hen Inn and Tavern. I'm Paul Jefferson, Master Tavern and Inn Keeper and owner too." His small, dark eyes twinkled in the candlelight. "Will you be needing lodging or a bit of hot tea or coffee and food?"

"Truth be told, Master Jefferson, I'm waiting for a coach from the Gerard House, thank you. I'll only ask for a place to sit and wait." She kept her smile.

His smile faded as he shifted his gaze to the floor and then back to Constance. "The Gerard House, Miss?" He shook his head slightly. "Been a long time since anyone stopped here on the way to Gerard House."

Oh, lovely, thought Constance. Was she going to get stuck in this desolate place all by herself? Her uncle had assured her that the Gerards would provide transportation from the inn to Gerard House.

She offered a weak smile to hide her discomfort and growing apprehension. "Thank you, Mr. Jefferson, but I'm certain my coach will arrive soon. It has all been arranged." She motioned to one of the tables. "May I have a seat? And I could actually use a cup of hot tea after all."

She had precious little coin left to her name, but if the tavern keeper was in need of a paying guest, then she'd have to sacrifice and pay up.

Paul Jefferson eyed her a few seconds more, then broke out in a broad smile, leading her toward the nearest table with two chairs.

"Please pardon this old man's ill manners, Miss Beechum. By all means, have a seat and I'll have Claire bring your tea." He pulled out the chair for her. "I'd be remiss if I didn't offer the apple knocker. It's our house specialty and the best in the colonies."

She settled into the chair. "No, just tea, thank you." Constance didn't want even a tinge of alcohol in her system when showing up for a job she desperately needed. The change in the innkeeper at the mention of Gerard House disturbed her. What did he know?

"Mr. Jefferson, have you dealings with the Gerards?"

He looked at her, his good humor again fading. "Oh yes, Miss, but not much. My cousin, Marguerite Maier, works as service maid several days a week at Gerard House. The poor lass, she lost her husband in the war. She came to live with me and the missus here. When Mr. Roger Gerard mentioned they were needing help at Gerard House several years ago, Marguerite saw her opportunity. A widow has to find work where she can." He began to fidget with his apron. "Roger Gerard graces us with a visit now and then. The Gerards live a very private life, you see, and want not much to do with the rest of Castine, except of course, for Lady Elizabeth when she was younger and in good health." He leaned forward, closer to her ear, as if his voice shouldn't be heard by any others in the room. "Keep to yourself at Gerard House and you'll be fit, Miss. Tell Marguerite I told you so."

He took off with a forced smile and disappeared through a wooden door in the back of the room. Claire brought her the hot tea in a cup of thick, plain off-white ceramic.

Constance had barely taken two sips of the too heavily sweetened tea, when the door of the inn burst open. A shower of snowflakes blew inside and a wide-shouldered man, bundled head to toe in heavy coat, boots, scarf, gloves and hat, strode in.

Hoping this was her escort to Gerard House, Constance eyed him with interest. She was eager to be on her way, to be finally safe in the warm hearth of Gerard House.

He noticed her and approached the table. "Might you be Miss Constance Beechum?"

"Indeed, I am." She noticed the man's heavy beard and moustache caked with snow.

He bowed. He didn't smile. "Wasn't sure you'd make it because of the snow and all. Master Edward and Roger bid me come and fetch you."

Constance hurriedly put down one pence for the tea on the table and followed him. He carried her two pieces of luggage quickly, strapping it down to the back of the small trap. Constance shivered at the thought of riding any long distance in such a small and open coach. While the trap did have the portable top up, it wasn't the most ideal traveling in this kind of weather. There was still light snow falling, but at least the wind had died down.

He helped her up on the seat next to him, pointing to a thick, folded blanket on the seat. "That'll keep you warm, Miss."

He hadn't needed to mention it. Constance quickly unfolded the rough blanket and draped it around her already shivering body. She couldn't stop trembling.

"Gerard House is a few miles ahead on a finger of land that sticks out into the sea. It shouldn't be too long, Miss." He flapped the reins on the horses hard. The trap lurched and they were on their way.

The small coach jostled along a winding road that seemed to disappear into an ever increasing curtain of whiteness. Once they traveled a distance in silence, the driver looked at her and tipped his hat lightly.

"The name's Grayson, Miss." He pointed to his beard. "Around here, they merely call me "Gray.""

Constance laughed, already feeling warmer.

"We should be able to see the house once we reach the top of the hill," he said.

"Are you the Gerard's driver?" Constance questioned.

"Oh, no, Miss. I'm a fisherman by trade. All my family lives off the sea. But I did work for the Gerards for a spell years ago. Anyway, the Masters Edward and Roger, they don't keep a regular driver anymore. They keep a couple of horses and hire from the town when there's need for a coach and such."

Constance thought that odd. With the Lady Gerard being so ill, why would the Gerard's not have at least a servant in waiting should they need to fetch help from the town since Gerard House was so far away. Why were they so secretive and unfriendly? She wasn't too fond with the idea of being so alone in a big house that was so isolated.

"Who lives at Gerard House?" she asked.

"Beside the sick Lady Elizabeth, there's Mr. Edward Gerard, his younger brother, Roger, Mr. Edward's wife, Catherine, and a servant girl who comes three or four days a week or so. They let go of Mrs. Winters, the old cook last year. Lady Elizabeth is mighty sick and needs constant looking after. Mrs. Gerard isn't the kind to do it, so I imagine that's why they hired you." He paused. "The Gerards are funny with keeping to themselves. They don't care much for strangers in the house."

Constance noticed his dark eyes appraising her. "I'd keep a watch on Mr. Roger, Miss. He's a ladies' man."

At that moment, the light wind seemed to die down completely and the curtain of snow parted like the curtains on opening day at the playhouse. Gerard House was monstrously large; a three story Federal that perhaps in its heydays had boasted great beauty and grace, but Constance was shocked at the decay of the house. In the distance, it stood dreary and grey at the edge of a towering cliff. Just behind it, she caught a glimpse of a tall lighthouse. But there was no light at the top. It was stony and dark, like the house.

As quickly as the wind had died, it increased with even more intensity. Constance wrapped the blanket tighter around her.

"The Gerard's no longer use the third floor. They've locked it up tight," Gray said.

Constance couldn't control the chill deep inside her. Gerard House made her colder than the snow. "I'm so cold, Gray."

"Once you get good, hot food and in front of a roaring fire, Miss, you'll do better."

The road took a turn away from the sea and guided them through a small parcel of woods, the giant oaks thick with snow. Constance was starting to feel fatigued by the rough journey. Numb from the snow and hungry, she was anxious to be out of the weather and safe inside Gerard House.

15

She was ready to question Gray on how near they actually were to the house when suddenly, out of nowhere, she saw several figures appear through the falling snow on the side of the road.

Constance grabbed hold of Gray's arm. "What—" She nearly screamed, but the three men darted across their path. The horses reared on their hind legs, spooked. The trap skidded off to the side, nearly tipping over.

This time she did scream and buried her face in her hands. She felt the tarp sway. She could still see those terrifying figures in her head—so large and so faceless.

It took Gray only a few moments to calm the horses down and get the trap back on the road. "We're all fine, Miss," he said.

Constance dared to take a look at the road in front of them again. The figures were gone. "What could they be doing out here in weather like this?" She was still trying to catch her breath.

"Deer," Gray answered and snapped the reins, the horses starting briskly up the road again with no resistance.

His answer surprised her. "Deer?"

He nodded without looking at her. The trap finally cleared the woods. She sensed he was lying and realized that the three men had worn cowls. Deeply hooded cowls.

That was why I couldn't see their faces and why I thought they were so large. She wanted to question the old man further, but a burst of icy cold wind hit her hard and left her speechless.

"Gerard House just yonder," Gray said, pointing.

Constance wasn't willing to forget those hooded men. "I think you know those were men back there on the road, Gray, not deer." She nearly had to scream above the strong wind. "You saw them too."

He faced her abruptly. His dark eyes shone like shiny onyx. He suddenly slapped the reins hard on the backs of the horses and hunkered down even further into his high collared coat.

16

She was more frightened by what she saw in Gray's eyes than by anything he could have uttered. For the briefest of moments, she had stared into the eyes of a man and looked into the depths of his soul. There dwelled fear and terror. She trembled now, clearly remembering what she had seen.

CHAPTER 3

Gerard House suddenly loomed out from the diminishing snow and the quickly approaching dark. One minute, there was nothing but the snow, and then the large, impressive house appeared before them. The image of the stately mansion was as fearsome as the Nor'easter that continued to batter the east colonies and the sea.

Constance had imagined the manor an elegant place by the sea, but the house before her, while large, was ill-kept and run down. It was a three-story Federal-style structure with tall, looming columns; but the paint was chipping and some of the windows needed cleaning, with their shutters hanging loose and lopsided in some of the third floor windows.

Sweet Lord, where has my uncle deposited me? Constance lamented silently. No candlelight flickered through any of the windows, yet she felt a chill as she distinctly thought she had been watched by prying eyes.

Gray jumped off the tarp. "I'll call for Master Edward or Roger."

She watched as he walked to the door and grabbed a brass knocker. He smashed it three times against the base plate, the sound echoing in the gathering darkness. Gray turned back to glance at her and then diverted his attention back to the door.

Constance couldn't control the shiver that went through her body. She wrapped the blanket even tighter around herself. Was it the cold or the house causing the chill? She had to get all the suspicious thoughts about Gerard House out of her system. This was to be her home, at least for some time. She had no idea how ill Elizabeth Gerard was, but as long as she required care, Constance would have the run of Gerard House; free room and board and food. That was far better than what she had left behind in Boston.

Constance eyed the door, watching as it opened slowly. Gray spoke to whoever was on the other side and looked back at her. As the door swung wider, she saw that there were two men, one holding a hurricane lamp. From this distance, the light was too feeble for her to make out his features.

"Go on inside, Miss," Gray said as he came back to the trap. "I'll take your luggage for you." He helped her down.

Constance didn't want his help but feared she might slip in the wet snow. Gripping his hand, she gently stepped away from the trap and whispered, "Thank you," then hurried up the flight of steps.

The orange, sickly glow from the lamp cast long, quivering shadows in the open doorway. She mounted the short steps to enter Gerard House and quickly glanced around. It was dark inside. Without formality, she breathlessly introduced herself to the two strangers facing her.

"Weren't you taught to curtsy when introducing yourself?" the man holding the lamp asked.

Constance fumed. She was tired, hungry, nervous and bitterly cold from her grueling journey, not to mention the unnerving incident on the way, and the ominous atmosphere that greeted her. She was in no mood to handle this man's ridicule.

"Have you, Sir, forgotten your manners on how to be civil?" she snapped back, looking straight at him.

"How can you respond to that, dear brother?" the other man questioned.

"No one spoke to you, you fool."

Gray went past them with her luggage. "Where should I put these, Master Edward?" he asked the man who had been so rude.

"Set them down there. Roger will attend to them."

Gray walked out without speaking another word, not even a good night to any of them.

"Close the door quickly," Edward Gerard urged his brother.

Edward Gerard was a short and unimpressive man. From what she could see in the poorly lit foyer, both men wore dark colored tailcoats and satin waistcoats with light-colored cravats. Roger Gerard's buff trousers tucked into his brown leather boots, and Edward wore dark pantaloons with black shoes. Edward wasn't much taller than Constance, who was barely five foot six inches; and he was stout to boot. He was the elder and his hair was more conservative, his sideburns cut shorter. On the contrary, his brother Roger Gerard was taller, leaner and far more stylish. He wore his hair tousled and tossed up in light curls with long, dark sideburns. Neither man looked to be older than sixty, at least in the dark. Roger was definitely much younger.

Constance untied the bow beneath her chin and removed her bonnet, dusting the rapidly melting snow from it.

"From your uncle's letter, I gather you are to look after my mother," Edward said.

"I am."

"He was foolish to send you. Foolish and illogical." He stopped and moved the light closer to examine her face. "I thought he'd have more common sense, being a man of the law, and that he would send an older, more experienced woman who won't get anxious about being locked up in the house for most of her days." His diatribe was delivered in such

20

a negative tone that Constance leaned away. "I don't expect you'll be staying with us long," he finished.

"I intend to do my job for as long as I'm needed," Constance answered curtly.

Roger's footsteps came from behind them. In spite of her resolve to not allow her overwrought state to betray her, she took a glance over her shoulder.

"Catherine, my wife, is upstairs with Mother. Only Roger and myself are downstairs," Edward announced.

Constance nodded. Like that was supposed to comfort her.

The hall through which they walked echoed with their footsteps. It was so huge and empty, that the lamp did not reach into every corner. Constance wondered. Why was Gerard House so sparse of furniture and candles for light?

Edward led her to a large, rectangle table. A place was already set, and several trays of food and a cup sat waiting.

"After you have some dinner," he said, "Roger will show you to your room. It is unfortunate that the maid has the day off and my wife is sitting with my mother." He put the lamp on the table and turned to his brother who stood almost hidden in the shadows. "You will see that Miss Beechum finds everything to her liking."

"Delighted," Roger said.

"I want no problems," he scolded his younger brother.

"I couldn't guess what you could mean, Brother," Roger said with a laugh.

"You know what I'm saying." Edward's voice was harsh. "Miss Beechum is a guest here."

"Of course, Brother, and a lovely one at that." Roger's gaze bore into Constance.

"When will I be able to see Mrs. Gerard?" Constance undid the buttons of her ratty coat and placed it atop one of the chairs.

"I will inform my mother that you have arrived, but you will not see her until tomorrow."

"I won't mind tending to her tonight."

21

"I care little what you mind or don't mind," Edward growled. He took off without another word and disappeared into the dark shadows of the great hall. Somewhere in the darkness, Constance heard a door open and slam shut.

She sighed and sat down, weary and apprehensive of her new surroundings. The hunger that had nibbled at her stomach before suddenly was gone. All she wanted was to lay her head on a pillow and sleep, or weep, until she passed out. Her bosom heaved from the tears she held back.

She looked up to suddenly find Roger staring at her. His eyes burned with more fire than the flame of the lamp. Constance felt uncomfortable that he had full view of her. Her modest dress pushed her full breasts against a deeply cut neckline.

"If you don't mind, Mr. Gerard, but you are making me most uncomfortable."

He smiled. "My pardon, dear lady, I meant no disrespect. But you are a very attractive woman. I never would have guessed that Barrister Merriweather hid away such beautiful relatives."

"I was hired," Constance answered hastily, "because of my professional capabilities and for no other reasons." She crossed her fingers and hoped that lie never had to surface. She reasoned that caring for an ailing older woman shouldn't be beyond her capabilities.

"I do so admire a woman with courage who hits back with attitude." He exclaimed in appreciation. "So many of your kind are such docile, uninteresting creatures. It gives me hope to see there are still some among you who are different."

Constance studied him silently. There was no denying that he was handsome. He was manly, not at all like the dandies. He was taller than his brother and broad of shoulder with a narrow waistline. His tailcoat fit him to a stitch. If he was hinting at any romance, he would abruptly learn that she had no interest in his manhood.

"I am quite certain, Miss Beechum, that we will get along quite well," he said confidently.

Constance contemplated her food.

"By the way, don't allow Edward to bother you," he continued, "You'll need your strength to deal with Mother."

"I'm afraid I've lost my appetite. I would, however, like a cup of hot coffee."

"That's coffee in the silver pot." He pointed to an elaborately ornate etched silver pot on the table.

She poured herself a full cup and asked if Roger would join her. He declined.

"Why is your brother Edward so upset at my arrival?" Constance dropped two cubes of sugar in her coffee.

"He's in a bit of a huff because he believes the entire family fortune will be his and his alone." Roger gestured. "He is impatient for Mother to die so he can become the Master of Gerard House."

Constance nearly choked on the coffee. "How dreadful! And for you to be so cavalier about it."

Roger laughed. "Oh, it isn't as bad as it sounds. Mother is quite old and has lived a long and generous life. And besides, Edward really won't be getting much."

Constance didn't understand. "I was under the impression that your family is very wealthy."

The raucous laugh that echoed from Roger's lips wasn't a cheerful one. "Look around, dear lady, we have seen better days! The house is in disrepair, our bank account needs constant watching, and none of us are willing to do what it takes to turn our fortune around. It all started going downhill when my father put his money and support behind King George on the wrong side of the war. Always a loyalist Whig, he continued his folly until his death, just to keep his business investment with England."

If that was so, Constance thought, the talk of blockades and war could not bode well for the Gerards.

23

"Then I'm to guess you're not too keen on what is happening between the colonies and England?"

He shook his head. "Most of the Gerard fortune was made in the shipping and exporting of lumber to the English. At one time, we had a fleet of ships that carried the lumber to the British. But alas, the ships are all gone, sold to help pay the house costs."

"Can't you or your brother find suitable business pursuits? Surely, with your family name, the opportunities are there."

This time, Roger did not laugh heartily.

"Oh, no, my dear Miss Beechum. My future is in the hands of my dear mother. What is left of the Gerard money and land will be put to good use at the local track." His eyes twinkled. "I'm betting my way will get me more."

Constance thought this good looking ladies' man quite a waste. She finished her coffee and rose from the table. "I would like to go to my room now. I am very exhausted."

Roger grabbed the lamp from the table. "You'll love your room. It's at the end of the west wing overlooking the sea and the mouth of the small cove."

"Is my room close to Lady Gerard's?" she asked as she walked beside him.

"Well, close enough."

"And where are Edward's and your rooms?'

"In the east wing. It is the newer part of the house."

As they passed along the wall of the great hall, the lamp's flickering flame danced upon the bottom part of a large painting. Constance paused but it was too dark to see more of it.

"It is a portrait of my mother in the prime of her life," Roger explained. "One of a few paintings that hasn't been sold to meet expenses."

A few moments later, they were at the long flight of stairs leading to the second floor. Constance followed Roger closely. There was definitely a shortage of candles at Gerard House. Surely, they could afford candles, or at least make some themselves. She wondered if she had merely traded living in her own poverty for someone else's life of poverty.

Gerard House filled her with trepidation. Nor could she erase the image of the three hooded figures from her mind. She still saw them dashing out of the falling snow and racing across the road, scaring herself and the horses into a frenzy. And now, the dark, sparse interior of Gerard House made her fear that perhaps she'd been foolish in accepting Uncle Merriweather's job offer blindly, trusting that he would not put her in peril. Had she put her life in jeopardy?

"I don't believe you've heard a word I've said," Roger commented irritably.

"I am sorry, but I am quite weary from my travels." Had he been talking?

"Forgive me," Roger said gallantly. "I should be more perceptive of your mood and exhaustion." He took a step toward her. "The room is just a short way down this corridor."

Constance moved to follow him when she suddenly got the eerie sensation that someone else was observing her. She looked over her shoulder and down to the bottom of the stairway, where she spotted another lamp glowing. In its flickering light, she saw Edward, his face upturned toward her. His expression revealed such an overwhelming hate that she could not squelch the startled cry of alarm that erupted from her lips.

Roger rushed to her side. "What is wrong, Miss Beechum?"

Numb from the fear-provoking gaze on Edward Gerard's face, Constance could not speak, but only point down to the bottom of the stairs.

"There is nothing there," Roger declared. "Look for yourself."

"No, I prefer not to."

"Please, believe me, you have nothing to fear."

She managed a nod. "I do believe you," she whispered. "Now please, take me to my room."

25

They had barely left the head of the stairway when Constance heard the whine of the wind outside as it pounded against the walls of the house. The lantern light illuminated the corridor, showing nothing more than a vaulted passageway with scattered chairs and mirrors here and there. It seemed to extend forever into the darkness. It was so black and devoid of candlelight that Constance could not tell where the hallway ended.

"Here is your room, Miss Beechum," Roger said, bending over as she stepped inside.

She moved no further. The room was as devoid of frills as the rest of Gerard House. There was a high canopied bed set with its headpiece against the far left wall. Opposite the bed was a smallish bureau of dark wood. A rough-shaped dowel set in a niche between two faces of the wall could serve as a place to hang her clothing. Roger deposited her two pieces of luggage on the bed, lit several candles and placed them in silver candleholders on the top of the bureau.

"Marguerite, our maid, comes in tomorrow. I'll have her tidy the room up a bit for you."

"Thank you, Mr. Gerard." As Constance moved further into her room, she noticed the large window. The wind outside crashed against it with a full fury.

"Don't you worry your pretty head," Roger assured her. "These windows have withstood worse."

"I'm sure they have, but I've not been here." She walked to the window and checked to see if it was still snowing. It was too dark to see anything. She turned to find Roger standing at the fireplace.

"The fire will get going soon," he said. "It should warm you up and cheer you."

Constance suddenly realized that there had been no fire in the dining room. *Perhaps if there had been, I would have felt better.* Roger finally had a good blaze going and several pieces of kindling were burning bright. She thanked him.

"There should be enough wood to last the night," he said.

"I'll be fast asleep and won't need to worry about the fire." She looked around her room with more cheer this time and noticed a small commode off to the side with a pitcher and a bowl sitting atop it. Was there water in the pitcher? She was too embarrassed to ask.

"You can see down to the cove from your window. It is just on the other side of the lighthouse. The cove and the lighthouse are called Lighthouse Pointe."

She had noticed the lighthouse on the way. "I saw there was no light in the lighthouse when we came in. Is it not functioning?"

Roger shook his head slightly. "I'm afraid not. We had to dismantle the lens elements to sell the glass pieces and copper casing."

The Gerard's were in worse shape than she feared. What could there possibly be left for anyone in Lady Gerard's Will? Constance stiffened as a more pressing dilemma presented itself to her. Was she any better off in a forsaken, run-down mansion with less than friendly strangers than in the boarding house in Boston?

"Well, I'm certain it is a wonderful sight," she said somewhat brashly, "but if you don't mind terribly, I would very much like to get to bed." She began to walk toward the door, expecting Roger to take his leave on her command. But he suddenly grabbed her arm and spun her around toward him. She struggled valiantly but she could not get free.

"I did not expect such a pretty nurse for my mother," he said arrogantly. "You certainly surprised my brother Edward as well. He thought your uncle would hire some old bitch with a wrinkled dry face but instead, he sent us his lovely niece." He tossed his head and laughed heartily.

"Please let me go!" Constance attempted to break his hold on her.

"Come now, Miss Beechum...Most ladies don't act this way when they are in *this* gentleman's arms." They continued to struggle and he jerked her body against his. "We'll never get this to work if you act like this," he purred in her ear.

"That is for certain," she answered angrily. "This will not work!"

He pursed his lips. "It will get tedious if I have to wrestle you to bed each time—"

"Don't you dare!"

Oblivious to her protestations, Roger said "I have known wenches who did like it rough."

Constance suddenly stopped her resistance.

"Now, now, that is so much better," he said with satisfaction. His face lowered toward hers but without warning, Constance ripped her nails across his cheek. He jumped back in shock, howling with pain. "You won't do that again, you bitch!" He held one hand to his bleeding face.

Finally free from his strong arms, Constance grabbed the tongs from the fireplace and inched backward toward the window. "I'm demanding you leave now." She said it with a courage she didn't actually feel.

Roger pulled a handkerchief from his sleeve and applied it to his cheek. "You don't think I intend to leave this room without retribution, do you?" He lunged for her again.

"I tell you, I won't hesitate to use these," Constance threatened. "If you come any closer, I most surely will!" She held out the tongs toward him and waved them in at his face. The shadows that the fire cast on the walls made the iron forceps look like giant torture devices. In her emboldened state of mind, they could be deadly.

Constance had no doubt she could use them to defend herself from bodily harm. She had already learned how to fend for herself. The heat from the fire made her throat and lips feel parched.

Roger did not remove his eyes from the tongs. "We will finish this another time," he said, inching backwards. "I am a patient man."

"You'd best not wait," she told him menacingly.

28

"I bid you good night, dear lady."

Constance sighed with relief and rested the tongs against the hearth. Almost immediately, Roger was upon her again, having rushed across the room. He brutally slammed her and pinned her arms against the wall, forcing his lips upon her own.

"Enough of that!" Edward's voice rang loudly through the room. "I will not have it in this house!"

Roger released her immediately and whirled around to meet his brother's eyes.

"I was a fool to trust you. I should have known better." Edward was furious and his face twisted in a rage. "Get out of this room instantly! And rest assured Mother will hear of this!"

Roger only nodded before he briskly left the room.

"Hurry!" Edward followed him out, not even looking at Constance or apologizing.

Constance ran for the door and secured the bolt. Totally exhausted, she threw herself on the bed and sobbed. She did not feel safe at Gerard House. Why did men assume they could have their way with any woman who was unmarried?

She cried and cried until she succumbed to exhaustion and fell asleep.

An intense chill woke her from her slumber. She awoke unsure of where she was, but slowly recognized her room in Gerard House. She took time to fully take in her surroundings. The fire was nearly out.

She got up and added two more large pieces of wood on the andirons. The candles Roger had lit were down to near nothing, hardly offering any illumination. She had to light two fresh candles to replenish the old ones in the candleholders.

What time was it? She suddenly realized how quiet it was. The wind outside had lessened considerably since she'd fallen asleep. She stepped to the window and looked outside. It had stopped snowing and the night was crisp and clean. Constance could see the twinkle of stars in the clear sky. She figured it wasn't near dawn yet.

The cold from the window chilled her. Moving away from the drafty window, she prepared to undress and get ready for bed. The fire in the fireplace heated the room and removing her dress and undershift felt good. Naked, she worked her way to the commode where she located a fresh piece of cloth. Constance washed herself with the water in the pitcher. It was so cold that goose bumps formed over her whole body. She dried herself quickly and, still shivering, she pulled out her long-sleeved nightgown and slipped it over her head. In seconds, she was curled up in the bed beneath heavy blankets.

Her gown rode up high on her thighs and her skin was chilled by the cold sheet. She shivered and thought to request a bed warming pan in the morning.

"That's assuming I stay here," she said aloud to herself. The thought of staying on at Gerard House was now far less appealing. She was confident she could handle Roger Gerard, but Edward was still a mystery to her—and she hadn't even met Catherine, his wife. The house was dark and oppressive and she continued to doubt if this had been a good idea.

She was having trouble sleeping. Constance turned her gaze to the window. It still wasn't light and the darkness seemed even heavier outside. Still fully awake, she left the bed and stepped on the cold stone floor to the window. Her heart sank. Snow had started to fall again, but not as heavy as when she had first arrived. The snow looked like a thin veil of wispy, white flakes. Even so, she could see some stars when she looked up.

Constance was just about to return back to her bed when she glanced out to the cove by the lighthouse. At first, she thought what she saw was a falling star. She closed her eyes and wished that she might one day find a true love. She hoped for a confident woman who would not be afraid of what love and commitment might bring. That wish brought a smile to her face. It was in quiet times like these that she thought of Lily, but Lily had not been that woman.

Constance opened her eyes and looked out at the cove again. She was shocked this time to not only see several lights swinging to and fro, but that the lighthouse had a bright light weakly emanating out into the black ocean! The lights in the cove seemed to blink and move in response to the light in the lighthouse. She watched in awe as the lights continued to wave back and forth, and suddenly vanished.

Constance rushed back to the bed and flung the cover over her head. *I should have turned around and gone back to Boston as soon as I saw those hooded men on the road! Now there are mysterious lights where there shouldn't be any!*

She managed to fight off the fear gnawing at her insides and eventually drifted off to sleep, although there was no peace in her dreams. They were filled with strange and terrible shadows who tried to attack her throughout the night.

CHAPTER 4

Edward held the candelabra out into the darkened hall as he walked beside Roger. When they stopped at the head of the stairway, Roger said that he was tired and was going to his room.

"You are not going anywhere," Edward said angrily. "You will accompany me to downstairs. Catherine is awaiting us. We need to discuss our intruder."

"Miss Beechum?" Roger shook his head, but followed his brother.

They both met Catherine Gerard downstairs and they joined her at the exact same table where Constance had taken coffee upon her arrival.

Edward placed the candelabra in the center of the table, its flickering candle light casting sinister shadows. His wife, Catherine, sat in one of the high back chairs. She had flaming red hair which was piled atop her head, with carefully prepared curls falling daintily across her forehead. Her silk dress was a pattern of small flowers with lace-trim at the cuffs of long sleeves. A shimmering sapphire necklace lay against her chest.

32

"There is wine on the side board," she said, lazily pointing at an antique decanter. She sighed. "I thought Elizabeth would never go to sleep."

Roger moved swiftly to fetch the crystal decanter and the matching wine glasses.

"I will have none of it," Edward said.

Roger shrugged. "As you wish."

Catherine nodded and reached for a glass. Roger poured himself a generous amount of wine and half a glass for his sister-in-law.

Edward eyed each of them closely. He knew both his brother and his greedy wife were eager for something from Elizabeth Gerard. For generations, the whispers and rumors, even among family members, were that the Gerards were keepers of a great secret treasure trove. The rumor had seeped into the conversations among tavern goers and local Castine families. The story was that a great treasure was discovered by Jeremiah Gerard sometime during the early 1700s while he was at sea. While the fortune the Gerards held up front and out in the open for the whole world to see was formidable, and allowed them to become one of New England's most prosperous and upstanding families, the treasure was always hidden from site and from conversation. Still, all three of them knew that whoever controlled the Gerard family, and money, was also keeper of the treasure secret.

Though Edward had never seen his mother's Will, he suspected—no, wished—that she had not bequeathed any of the family fortune to his useless brother. Roger had been an embarrassment. He was a rogue, more interested in gambling his life and money away in games, women and drink. He stayed away for long periods of time, only to return when he needed cash to worm his way out of gambling debts or to pay off a pregnant wench.

And now that their mother was approaching death's door, Edward felt sure Roger was only here to sniff out his winnings. Like a vulture. It was not out of kindness or love, that was certain. He was merely after more money so he could return to his ill begotten ways.

"What are your thoughts, Edward?" Catherine asked, taking a sip of her wine.

"You do seem lost in thought," added Roger, pouring himself a second glass.

"You were so busy guzzling your wine, I'm surprised you noticed."

Roger smiled mischievously. "A good drink is never distracting." He raised his glass in a mock toast to his brother.

"I would take care it does not dull your common sense," Edward replied venomously.

"Well, my common sense tells me you lust for the pretty wench upstairs as much ad I do." His gazed shifted to Catherine.

She glared at her husband. "And still you've not learned your lessons, Edward. Soon, we'll be running out of room at the family cemetery."

Edward was taken aback by Roger's accusation and his wife's cold contempt.

"I have no interest in Miss Beechum. My attention is focused only on our situation with Mother."

"Oh, come now, brother—a lovely woman like that, and single too, could delight any hot-blooded man. Or perhaps now you are preferring your own and their charms?"

Edward started out of his chair, face in a rage.

"Stop it, both of you! Roger, you push Edward too far," Catherine said. "Edward, sit down. He has nothing to entertain himself with but to incite your anger. Don't give him the pleasure."

Edward sat back, scowling. "One day, you will push me too far."

"I was only jesting, Edward." Roger laughed it off. "Come now, have a drink with us. Why not celebrate the arrival of Miss Beechum? The fair damsel will add color to this drab old house."

34

"I did not ask you both here to get drunk."

Roger only stared at him blankly.

"We need to discuss our—"Edward paused, "—our mutual future."

Roger set his wine glass on the table. "You are acknowledging that Mother could be choosing me as Master of Gerard House? How surprising." His lips curled in a wicked smile.

"Oh, heavens, no. I merely am suggesting you might be left in my charge, monies included. Mother never approved of the way you chose to live your life and wasted the Gerard money."

Roger said nothing. Edward looked at his wife and then back at Roger. "We must all act in concert."

"Your mother has but little time left," Catherine said, her dark eyes glittering in the candlelight.

"She seemed bright when I visited her this morning," Edward said.

"I suspect her illness permits her some hours respite from the pain she is enduring. When I left her a while ago, I had to give her more of the draught to help her sleep."

"She is slowly dying, our dear mother," Roger said.

"That is my thought," Catherine said.

"I agree with you both," Edward said. "I am wracked with pity each time I see her in that bed."

"What has any of this to do with our mutual future?" Roger asked impatiently. "Frankly, all this talk of Mother's agony makes my stomach twitch with illness."

"I am just stating," Edward continued, "that I sometimes think it would be quite merciful to shorten her length of suffering."

Roger jumped up from his chair. "I will not be part of what you suggest—"

"Sit down!" Edward demanded. "Do you imagine that I would risk entertaining the remotest chance that Mother's death should appear to have come about from something

35

other than a natural cause? You are a bigger fool than I even imagined." Edward shook his head. "It would have been easy for me to dispatch Mother's earthly body to the heavenly world if I desired. But what if, by some chance, my act of mercy was discovered for what it was? Mercy! More than likely, I would stand trial for my life and you, dear brother, would squander the treasure and sell off Gerard House. No, merciful though the act would actually be, it would not be seen as such. Mother is in the hands of providence, which will remove her in its good time."

Roger reached for more wine. "Well, it seems to me all this talk has led us nowhere. I'm quite bored."

Catherine shook her head slowly. "The issue," she said, barely controlling her patience, "is whether or not we're interested in staying the hand of providence or letting it whisk Elizabeth away in the shortest time possible."

"My dear sister-in-law, please come to the point."

It was Edward who answered. "Mother should not have the benefit of too much care or comfort." He glared at Roger.

"So you mean you don't want Miss Beechum to—"

"That is precisely what we mean. She has to go quickly," Catherine finished.

Roger leaned back into the chair, wine glass in hand, then suddenly burst out in laughter.

"I fail to see the humor in the situation," Edward told him.

"I thought it was you who called for Miss Beechum. Surely, once Mother sees her, she will be cheered and certainly gain energy and time before her demise. She is a pretty face, indeed."

"I did not send for anyone. Mother wrote the letter to William Merriweather, our family barrister, and had Marguerite post it for her. If I had known, I would have stopped it."

"And if I'd been there in the room with Elizabeth," Catherine said, "I could have torn it up as soon as I left the room."

36

"Perhaps I might be able to aid us all in our endeavor." Roger got up and began pacing. "I've always had a way with women. I've never known a woman who was not foolish once she believed herself to be in love. I can make sure our Miss Beechum is too preoccupied to be of any service to Mother."

"Be careful, brother, that you are not the one played for a fool."

Roger sat back down and finished pouring the last of the wine. "Well, I enjoy having a young woman other than that dreary maid here." He lifted the glass in toast. "She will make a dull, dark place like Gerard House seem attractive for a bit, at least."

"She has to go," Edward said forcefully.

"Surely you do not wish Mother lowered into the cold grave so eagerly?"

"I agree with my husband. It is time she went."

Roger looked at Catherine slyly. "For once, my dear, you agree with your husband. How refreshing. Patience. It will happen soon enough. The hand of providence will take Mother, regardless of whatever comforts Constance Beechum will offer."

"No, she must go," Edward repeated.

Roger drained the wine in his glass. "I'll not have any part of it."

"Do you wish to keep that woman here to satisfy your sick lust and risk waiting who knows how long living only on Mother's allowance?"

"Presently, Miss Beechum is the perfect reason. She is a tasty morsel."

"Those scratches on your cheek should be a reminder that your charms will not work on Miss Beechum."

"But you forget," Catherine interjected, "that dear Roger likes them feisty."

"And that was only the first sally," Roger laughed. "Seldom is the castle breached with one assault. The fun is only just beginning. I aim to take her and it will be done subtly, by employing tried-and-true strategy."

"I promise, Roger, I will speak to Mother about your behavior," Edward threatened.

"By God, if you do," Roger countered, "I will be forced to tell her about this conversation."

"You idiot!"

"No more or less than you. I may win Constance Beechum, and perhaps she will impress Mother too. We will both be in Mother's good graces. Perhaps I am in a better position than you and Catherine." He stood up. "Good night, brother." He turned to Catherine. "Sister-in-law. Thank you for making this a very pleasant night indeed."

Edward turned from his brother in disgust. When Roger was gone, he turned to his wife.

"There is so much more involved than that pious fool understands."

Catherine got up and walked to put her hands on her husband's shoulders. "We must get that girl out of the way, you understand?"

He nodded in agreement. "I will find a way to remove her before she causes too much damage to our plans, even if she must be delivered to the coven for the final sacrifice."

Catherine reached over and took one of the candleholders on the table. "I can hardly wait to meet this ravishing creature that must meet her end. Mind you, Dear Husband, you must do away with her swiftly and don't get caught up in her heaving bosom. I don't need to remind you of what happened the last time."

She walked away, disappearing into the dark shadows.

CHAPTER 5

Elizabeth Gerard lay with her back propped up against several pillows. Her shrunken body seeming like that of a child in comparison with the oversized, canopied bed. She'd given up dressing up only to sit in bed, and instead wore a nightshirt with lacy trim at the collar and sleeves. She had blankets galore over her thin body and feet, which seemed to be eternally cold.

At her beside was a small brass bell that sat atop a beautiful wood-inlaid table. When she had need of Catherine, Roger, or Edward, she rang the bell until one of them heard her. Next to the bell sat her meal tray. She'd barely touched her lunch.

She'd spent the last hour reading the week-old newspaper account of President Madison's folly and dangerous plans to surge into the wilds of Canada. The United States was speeding headlong into war with the British again. Elizabeth didn't think the British would give up what they had won in Canada so easily. Madison counted on the help of the savages, but that was insanity. They would likely side with the redcoats. She knew that continued hostility with England and the beating of war drums could also do damage to the Gerard trade with the British.

Upset with the ongoing events, she flung the paper to the floor and rolled her head to the window. She could not see the snow or the ground with her view limited to a rectangular picture of iron grey sky. Seagulls breezed by every so often and then vanished from her sight. Yet, she delighted in seeing even the seagulls outside.

Elizabeth spent many hours daydreaming and looking outside the window since she had been confined to her bed. She enjoyed drifting off and playing once again in her past. In her youth, Elizabeth had been the envy of the girls in her circle. Rosy cheeks, full lips and hair a shimmering shade of chestnut, she had had more than her share of suitors and friends.

At times, Elizabeth's reverie caused her to smile at her own antics. She had been so foolish with some of the young gentlemen. When thoughts of Hugo, her husband, became too much to bear, she remembered the good times only. He had been a good man and a good husband, but the passion of love had never been present in their marriage. He spent so much time at sea that raising Roger and Edward had fallen completely on her shoulders. Roger was a disappointment. An immature man who still believes money is his privilege. And Edward's dark and angry disposition was even harder for her to bear.

He had followed in her footsteps and married a woman he didn't love at Hugo's urging.

Hugo thought Catherine Mathers the perfect match for Edward. Maybe Hugo had been in love with Catherine himself. Elizabeth had never been strong enough to confront him with the query. And that was why Edward dallied with every pretty maid that crossed the Gerard threshold, and why she'd had to spend a fortune covering up Edward's most dreadful affairs and the repercussions. That was also why Edward and Catherine's marriage was barren.

But Elizabeth remained a realist. She knew that she was a dying woman. The disease spared no one, rich or poor. It was rapidly spreading through her body, sometimes making it impossible for her to even lift her arms or legs. It was as if her body was dissolving. She mostly learned to live with the pain, though there were dark times when even the laudanum could not ease it. All she could do was bite hard on her hand to prevent from crying out. The seizures sometimes lasted too long.

She lay with her head still turned to the window, wishing and hoping that she would pay her a visit. Elizabeth understood the dangers of her visits but also delighted in the delicious game they both had played for so long. When she visited, together they spoke of what went on outside and the world.

Thinking about her caused Elizabeth to suddenly remember that her lawyer, William Merriweather, had been contacted to send a nurse. She remembered that Marguerite had written the missive for her and posted it. That seemed months ago. Why had she not come? Impatient to find out why Merriweather had not written or sent someone, she reached for the bell and began to ring it.

A slight, young woman with wavy hair, downcast green eyes and fair skin, came through the door.

"Marguerite, get Edward or Roger, but not Catherine."

Marguerite curtsied and rushed out to fetch Elizabeth's sons.

"Is anything wrong, Mother dear?" Roger asked, coming up behind the servant.

"Come inside," Elizabeth told him, and to Marguerite, "Find Edward, please."

Roger moved to her bedside. "Do you need your laudanum, Mother?"

"What I want to know is where you and Edward have been all day?"

Before Roger could answer, the door opened and Edward entered. Elizabeth eyed them both. They looked elegant in their tailcoats and cravats, but their faces betrayed their true nature. The stress of her illness and the battle for the Will was etched in the dark circles under their eyes and haggard complexions.

"Neither of you have visited with me today," she said accusingly.

"There are matters that need taking care of, Mother," Edward said.

"Am I then to remain like a zombie and rot here without any company except the comings and goings of Marguerite?"

Neither Roger or Edward had a response.

"Has anyone seen Mr. Kane?"

"We had a terrible storm yesterday," Roger said. "He might not be able to leave the lighthouse cottage for several days."

Elizabeth stared at him. "Mr. Kane always remembers to visit me and I daresay, he wouldn't let inclement weather break his visits." She turned to Edward. "Has there been any mail?"

"No, as Roger said, the storm was severe. I do not believe the post will arrive for several days."

Elizabeth sighed heavily. "Send someone to Castine, then, as soon as the weather permits. Perhaps Mr. Merriweather has written me regarding the nurse."

"But she has already arrived," Roger blurted.

"You fool!" Edward exclaimed.

Elizabeth set her gaze from one to the other. "Why did you keep this from me?"

"She came in late last night," Edward explained.

"And where is she?"

"In her room right now."

"Why did you not bring her to me earlier?"

"I thought—"

"You thought yourself Master of Gerard House already and that you could do what you wanted, eh? Well, Edward, I am still very much alive and still mistress of the house."

"Of course, Mother," Edward answered in a monotone, "but I feel she is too young—and seeing how you lose your patience with Marguerite, I had hoped to see if we could get Mr. Merriweather to send an older, more suitable replacement. I only waited for a time when you felt well to announce her arrival since I could not send her away without your approval."

Elizabeth realized that she was growing less and less able to do for herself. Even though she personally would have preferred an older nurse, perhaps a younger woman with strength and verve would be better.

"You do not have to see her, you know," Edward quickly said. "I can tell her that it was a mistake and that you do not require her services after all."

"She is young, pretty and sturdy, Mother," Roger said.

"And a nurse?" Elizabeth asked.

"We are to assume."

"Mr. Merriweather must have been mad to send her," Edward said.

Elizabeth ignored her eldest son and continued to study Roger. "Come, Roger, let me see the other side of your face clearly."

Roger hesitated, briefly putting his hand over the scratches.

"Turn, I say."

Roger slowly turned his scratched cheek to his mother.

"So, you've found her agreeable, I see. But alas, she did not. Too bad she didn't do worse. You haven't changed your ways and I do fear you never will." She sighed deeply. "I want to meet her."

"Mother," Edward pleaded, "it will be a waste of time and cause you much stress. It will tire you immensely. I can tell her to return to Boston."

"I will see her, Edward."

"Look at you," Edward continued, "you are even now allowing yourself to become angry over a young wench whom I believe lacks the necessary skills to administer you proper care."

Elizabeth stared her son down. Her voice was controlled but angry. "You will bring her here."

"She should not stay." Edward stood stubbornly at his mother's bedside, his back straight.

Elizabeth managed to control her mounting rage. It would do her no good to get so weakened. "I did not insinuate that she would stay. Now, tell me why she should not stay."

Edward was at a loss for words. He pointed an accusatory finger at Roger. "Don't believe what this rogue tells you because he will try to make her his whore in this house."

Elizabeth raised a white, bushy eyebrow. "And since when has Roger's ways and women mattered to you?"

Edward's shoulders sagged in defeat. "There is just something not right about that woman. She bodes ill luck, I feel."

"Roger, do you feel the same about my new nurse?"

Roger slowly shook his head. "She bodes only great beauty and—"

"I can sense it," Edward said sternly. "You can sense only another conquest."

"Enough, the both of you," Elizabeth commanded. "Bring her to me, Edward, and never, as long as I have a living breath, withhold anything from me again."

"As you wish."

To Roger, Elizabeth said, "You stay away from my nurse and be a gentleman about it, for once in your life."

"Of course, Mother."

"Now, Roger, please light me some candles. It grows dark outside."

CHAPTER 6

Furious at the turn of events, Edward headed to his own quarters. He'd managed to put off Constance's request to see her patient for most of the day and had great hopes he would manage to convince his mother to send her away without even meeting her. Edward had felt sure he could convince his mother that it had been William Merriweather's mistake, but Roger had ruined everything.

He thrust his weight against the door of his room. Where the devil was Catherine? She was probably down in the sitting room working on her silly scrapbook. Good! The more his nagging wife was away, the better. He made sure his door was securely bolted. He hoped Catherine wouldn't come pounding on it.

He didn't trust his wife. Even though she was as greedy as he and wanted to share in the good fortunes of the Gerard treasure, she could just as easily put a knife in his back and run off with Roger instead. No, he didn't trust her.

He was determined to make Constance Beechum leave now, lest she succeed in prolonging his mother's life, thereby extending his waiting period for the day when he became Master of Gerard House and its treasure. "I will not have her interfere!" he swore out loud. "I will not endure the wait any longer. I cannot abide my brother here. He will be gone— banished—when I am Master."

Edward allowed himself to calm down after a few minutes. He moved to the far end of the room and ran his fingers over the seam of what appeared to be a simple panel of wall. Finding the slight, irregular spot he was searching for, Edward pressed in and the panel began to open. Edward stepped into a passageway. He lit a candle sitting atop a table at his side and watched the panel slide shut behind him.

He could hardly suppress a chuckle as he thought of how easily he had hidden the secret panel and its passageway from both his wife and brother. Slowly, he followed the corridor until he came to a flight of rickety, wooden steps. Halfway up, he stopped and cast his look eyes upward. He couldn't see much because the light of his candle was insufficient to illuminate more than a few feet before or behind him. He could, of course, have fetched the wretched nurse by conventional methods, but this way, he would have the delicious opportunity of entering her room quite unexpectedly, seemingly materializing out of thin air. He was anxious to see her as a real woman. The thought made him smile. What a chance to view a woman unguarded, in her own privacy! The possibility of witnessing her in all her nakedness coursed like bloody fire through his veins. The anticipation was agonizing.

He quickened his steps and continued up the steps. Once he reached the top, he snuffed out the candle and put it in an iron holder mounted on the wall. The blackness was suffocating and consuming. Edward groped along the wall surface until he found the big iron loop. His heart beat wildly as he pulled hard on the loop and a section of the wall slid open. His pulse throbbed in his neck as he stepped inside.

He was in her room, shielded from any portion of the room by the stonework of the fireplace. With caution, he peeked around the frame of the wall. His heart was pounding so hard, he felt sure the tantalizing young woman would find him out.

Constance stood at the window, leaning against the wall. She had an unhappy expression on her face, with her breasts rising and falling as if she were sighing. Edward inhaled in excitement. She suddenly moved and stood directly in front of the window. Now was his chance. He stepped from his hiding place and came up to stand squarely behind his unsuspecting prey.

CHAPTER 7

Constance had seen the small figure of a man in the distance where the cove lay, but as soon as she stepped in front of the window to watch him, she instead saw the reflection of Edward Gerard approaching behind her. She whirled around to face him.

"I knocked," he said, "but you did not respond."

"I heard no one knock," she said, eyeing him with suspicion and quite flustered by his sudden appearance in her room.

"Perhaps you were too caught up in your daydreaming."

Constance cast a look at the door behind him. It was closed. She couldn't suppress the chill that made her shiver.

"Mother is asking for you," Edward announced.

"Thank you." She gathered her composure, still disturbed that she'd heard no knock at her door. "Let me grab a shawl." She found a light woolen shawl in the dresser and threw it over her shoulders. "I'm ready to meet Lady Gerard."

Edward turned toward the door and bowed slightly. "After you, Miss Beechum," he said with a fake smile. He reached out and chivalrously opened the door for her.

Still wondering, Constance couldn't remember whether she had shut the bolt to her door or not.

"I think it is only fair to warn you," Edward said as they walked along the hallway, "it would be in your best interest to leave Gerard House."

Constance lost her patience. She'd spent a useless day in her room waiting to see Lady Gerard. Now she wasn't sure if it was because Elizabeth Gerard did not wish to see her or because Edward was bound and determined to prevent it.

"If that is what Lady Gerard wishes," she said curtly, "I will obey."

"You must understand that my mother is much too ill to know what is best for her."

Constance stopped. "Are you telling me that you speak for her, then?"

Edward shook his head slightly. "No, Madam, I speak for no one but myself. But you would be foolish not to consider seriously what I have said honestly."

"Well, Sir, consider yourself relieved from any responsibility for me," she shot back.

"So I am to assume you wish to remain exposed to my brother's aggressive overtures, then?"

"I believe he will think twice again before approaching me again in that manner."

"Do not delude yourself," Edward warned. "You are overmatched, dear lady. Roger will not stop until he has his way with you."

"I have said that I can handle Mr. Gerard, but frankly, Sir, I am growing increasingly concerned over your intentions."

"I am guilty only of trying to do you a service," Edward said, "but your manner clearly indicates you intend to place yourself in this position."

"My intentions," Constance said firmly, "are to care for my patient—your mother—if she wants me to. It is the job I came here to do. I am growing impatient and have no interest neither in your brother's childish importuning or Gerard

49

family matters. Now, may we continue to your Mother's room?"

Edward smiled slyly. "I hope you will not regret your obstinacy. Nevertheless, I will entreat once again, do not remain here. Gerard House can cause nothing but unhappiness or worse—"

Constance was surprised. Was that a threat? "Why the hesitation?"

His smile broadened. "No need to go further. You know the ultimate possibility. But I remain confident that you will come to your senses and be gone before then."

"Please, I wish to see Lady Gerard."

Edward nodded. "Of course. We can reach the new wing by way of the balcony above the foyer," he said. "I must warn you, however, that if you have a fear of heights, do not look over or approach the guard rails."

Constance walked beside him. As they crossed the narrow balcony, she admittedly controlled a desire to move closer to the edge and peer down. Had that been Edward's intent for the warning?

"I admire your self-control, Miss Beechum," Edward said as they had crossed the balcony. "Make sure you exercise it in the future as well."

Before she had a chance to respond, they had stopped in front of a large, ornate oaken door. He knocked several times before a weak voice inside bid them to enter.

"Here is Miss Beechum, your nurse," he said as they entered.

"What took so long?"

"I had not realized that such a long time had passed," Edward answered.

Elizabeth said nothing, but turned her gaze from Edward to Constance. "Well, come in and come closer, young woman."

Constance walked hesitantly to the foot of the bed.

"Over here, young lady," Elizabeth said, pointing to a spot near the side of her bed. "How do you expect me to see you

50

clearly?" She looked at Edward. "I will ring if I need you," she said, dismissing him.

He bowed slightly. "Of course, Mother." He withdrew quickly, closing the bedroom door behind him.

Constance looked at Elizabeth Gerard. There was little doubt she was a dying woman. The skin on her face was taut against her bony skull, pronouncing the skeletal look in grim detail. Her hands were bony and withered, and they shook like wind-tossed leaves. But there was still fire and life in her crystal blue eyes. The disease had not yet taken hold of her spirit.

"Are you merely going to stand there and gape at me, young woman?"

Her voice startled Constance from her thoughts. "Please forgive me. I'm terribly sorry."

"Have you never seen such a wreck as myself, Miss...?"

"Miss Beechum," she said. "Miss Constance Beechum." Constance curtsied.

"Well, how long do you think you'll be caring for me, Miss Beechum? Does my condition frighten you?"

"It really isn't up to me to comment on that, Lady Gerard. I am not a physician."

Elizabeth chuckled. "Well, of course not, child. I am not a fool to think someone of our sex or your age could be a doctor. I know you are here to nurse me until I no longer need any further assistance."

Constance knew her face was red. She felt the heat rush to her cheeks.

"So tell me, what made your uncle think you are qualified to take care of a dying woman?"

Constance had feared such a question. She had no formal training and now somewhat regretted putting herself in a position to have to resort to lies.

"I have nursed many old friends."

Elizabeth waved her response away with a bony hand. "Come stand closer," she said. "I can barely see you. My eyesight has suffered as well, and the light is so poor."

Constance moved closer to her side.

Elizabeth stared at her. "How old are you?"

"Twenty-four, but I have cared for several ill friends already."

The old woman continued to eye her steadily. "Then I am to assume you are no stranger to death?"

Constance didn't have to lie this time. She'd been with more than one starving woman in the streets as she died gasping her last breath.

"I've seen the shadow of Death," she answered softly, pushing away those memories and her own desires to meet death willingly. "I do not consider him to be more than a greedy caller."

"And you are not frightened of his being close at hand?"

"I've never thought of Death as an enemy. He follows God's will and I cannot challenge that."

"God's will?"

"Our lives and our deaths are in the hands of the Almighty." If only Lady Gerard knew how close she had been to blaspheming God with that bottle of sleep draught.

Elizabeth smiled a weak smile. "Indeed, child, I am wont to believe you are right. And what of your parents?"

"They are long dead, I'm afraid. My Uncle Merriweather and his wife are my last surviving kin. I was making do in Boston before uncle sent me to be your nurse."

Elizabeth studied for a moment longer. "My son Edward does not think you should stay on at Gerard House."

"He has made that clear to me."

"I should have known. Has he said anything else?"

"No."

"But Roger is sweet on you. He fights for you to remain," Elizabeth said with a smile. "And now I see why he feels so strongly about you."

Again, Constance felt her cheeks go flush.

"I must say, you are a fine scratcher."

Constance cast her gaze downward. "Lady Gerard, it is ultimately your decision whether I stay or leave," she said.

"And so it is," she answered. "I shall think about it and inform you of my decision in a matter of days. In the meantime, consider yourself my nurse and a member of the Gerard household."

"Yes, my lady," Constance answered with a polite curtsey.

"And enough of that "my lady" business. You will call me Elizabeth." She laughed. "Oh, but Edward will not be too pleased, I warn you. But don't worry, he is rarely pleased about anything these days, and his wife probably has much to do with that. Have you met Catherine?"

"I've not yet had that pleasure."

"Well, you've missed nothing and I doubt you will find it much of a pleasure. She thinks I trust her when she is caring for me, but I don't. And you shouldn't either."

"Is there anything I can do for you now, Elizabeth?"

"No, you may go, but tomorrow morning, you will begin your duties. Get Marguerite to assist you if you need help."

Constance nodded, but already her patient's eyes were closed, her mouth slack as she drifted to sleep. She quietly left the room.

The hallway was very dark except for a single candelabra at the end, where the staircase led down to the foyer. She regretted not having brought a candle from her room.

"Miss Beechum?" A woman's voice called from behind, in the shadows.

Constance turned to face a tall woman with deep red hair holding a candle in front of her. Her dark, high-waisted dress pushed an ample bosom nearly over the edge of the top. She eyed Constance with surprise and interest.

"I am Constance Beechum."

"Well, I am glad we've finally been able to meet. I'm Catherine Gerard, Edward's wife." Her eyes traveled the length of Constance's body. "I suppose you've met Elizabeth?"

"I've just left her resting. She's fallen asleep." Constance felt uncomfortable under the woman's extreme scrutiny.

"I've been taking good care of her, you should know. I truly do not understand why she felt she needed outside care."

Why is everyone hostile in this house? Why do they reject anyone outside of the Gerard family?

Constance desperately wanted to get away to her room. "If you will excuse me, Mrs. Gerard, I am very tired and I'd like to get back to my room. I am very pleased to have met you."

The woman in front of her nodded, never taking her eyes off Constance as she stepped away. "I'll send Marguerite to your room with fresh linens and towels. She's only here part of the week, so make sure she gets you enough of what you require."

Constance gathered her shawl about her shoulders and guided by candlelight, made her way carefully across the balcony and back toward the older part of the house and the safety of her room. However, as she walked closer to the edge of the balcony, she gave way to her temptations, paused, and looked down over the railing. She was filled with dread at the darkness below. She felt as if she were peering into a black pit. There was a floor below, she knew, yet it all seemed surreal.

Unable to stop herself, she bent further over the railing. Suddenly frightened, Constance jerked herself back and she ran the whole way back to her room in trepidation.

CHAPTER 8

Constance took dinner with Roger in the large dining room, but for once, many candles were burning brightly in the beautiful glass chandelier that hung over the table. She wondered about Edward and Catherine but didn't really care to inquire after their whereabouts.

Their conversation was mostly tedious pleasantries. The food, though not elaborate, was satisfying. There was an over-abundance of soup, meat and vegetables. It was rather too much food for Constance. Could it be that she had spent so many years barely existing on bread and cheese that she now felt guilty enjoying all this fare?

"Does Marguerite cook all this herself?"

"Marvelous, isn't she? Yes, since she's only here several days of the week, the food keeps for several days until she returns. We have food carted in on other days."

This all seemed rather odd to Constance. Why not hire a full staff and kitchen help as well. Were the Gerard's so distrustful of strangers that they preferred their food be brought to them from the village rather than hiring a staff to cook? Or were they that broke?

Marguerite was a thin, small framed young woman who moved at lightning speed. Her gaze was constantly focused on the floor. The one moment she cast a look at Constance, her clear, green eyes seemed filled with exhaustion. She wore a blue frock, white apron, a mop cap, and strands of her brown hair trailed behind her ears.

It wasn't until after Marguerite had served tea that Roger finally brought up his ill-mannered behavior. "You must know, Miss Beechum, that I meant you no harm." He lowered his eyes. "I merely wanted—"

"Please, don't bring the matter up," Constance interrupted. "I do not wish to discuss that event any further."

He nodded. "It would please me if you would accept my apology."

She studied him. She really did want to accept his apology and believed he was sincerely sorry, but she'd also learned enough about human behavior to not be so easily fooled by words or emotion.

"Let's just say, Mr. Gerard, that I have put the unfortunate incident behind me."

Roger brightened at her words. "Thank you, Miss Beechum," he said with great feeling.

Desiring to proceed to another subject, Constance mentioned that she'd finally had the opportunity to meet his mother.

"Mother can be difficult. How did your meeting go?"

"She agreed to give me her decision on whether I should stay in a day or so."

Roger leaned toward her and whispered. "Do you think she has much time left?"

Constance set her tea cup down. "I do not believe she has much time left." She, of course, didn't really know because she wasn't a nurse in reality, but the older woman had looked ghostly and frail.

"Oh, poor Mother," Roger sighed. He sat back in his chair. "Please do as much as you can to make her last days as comfortable as possible."

"That is what I am here for."

"I trust you will," he answered.

"Your brother Edward does not seem to agree with you, nor my ability to help your mother. In fact, he isn't at all pleased that I am here."

"Please don't judge him too harshly," Roger said. "He is weighed down with the great burden of mother's impending end and all that comes afterward."

Roger's manner and words were inconsistent with his actions and what he'd previously said regarding Edward the night before. Perhaps he'd had a change of heart. Constance found it difficult not to believe in Roger's sincerity. He was rather convincing. She imagined how easily a young lady could succumb to his honey-coated manners and his big brown eyes. His eloquent speech would surely be the winning touch for most women. It was such a shame that he was wasting his intentions on her.

"But Miss Beechum, let's not dwell on such unpleasant things as death." His demeanor was gay, and he had plastered a broad smile on his face. "Please tell me something of yourself."

Constance smiled. "I'm afraid there isn't much to tell," she said. "I'd much rather hear tales of your adventures."

He became excited. "I daresay, I have seen something of life, in places such as England, Paris and Spain."

"Oh," she said. "Business or pleasure?"

"Both. The Gerard family has long been dependent on the Crown for much of its exports. And I have enough adventures to make even an old soldier blush."

Constance was immediately sorry she had asked, but she patiently listened as he embellished his stories with great detail. Was he telling the truth? How was she to know, he had such a flair for the dramatic. His immaturity showed through in his tales when he always, as the dashing hero, was rewarded with a beautiful woman's kiss.

After some time, Constance grew tired. She stifled a yawn.

"Oh, but how astonishingly thoughtless of me, dear lady," he exclaimed. "Here I am prattling on like an old lady, forgetting that you've had a tiring day. Forgive me, please. I get carried away with my tales. I so rarely find willing listeners in this house."

"I am sorry, Mr. Gerard, but I am rather exhausted."

Roger stood up and walked around to help her with the chair. Suddenly, he took her hand and brushed a kiss upon it before he bid her a good night. "I can walk you to your room if you wish."

Constance, caught by surprise, certainly couldn't withdraw her hand, but she could decline his offer. She didn't want to fight him off again. Better not give Roger Gerard too much familiarity. She had no interest in him.

"Thank you, but no. Please finish your tea. I can find my way fine."

He only nodded.

Constance took leave of him and left the dining room. Tonight, the chandeliers in Gerard House were ablaze. All the gloomy shadows that seemed like inky ghosts when she'd arrived were gone. But now, she could see that the mansion, while at one time a beautiful house, had seen better days. Still, she welcomed the bright candlelight to show her the way back to her room.

Once she was in her room, she made sure she bolted the door shut. She'd had enough of unannounced visitors. Then she lit her own fire and several fresh candles that Marguerite had obviously brought in before she returned to her own house. She'd also left fresh linens on the bed. Constance hoped to talk more at length with Marguerite, but feared the poor woman was worked to death. She missed female companionship and her meeting with Catherine Gerard had been as distasteful as the meeting with her husband.

She had to admit that her chambers, when brightly lit, possessed a certain faded elegance and charm. She felt better than she had when first she saw the room. Constance hummed a tune as she slipped off her dress and then her shift.

After carefully washing and drying herself, she slipped into her nightgown and went to the window. It had stopped snowing earlier in the day and now a bright half-moon hung high against the deep, indigo sky. She loved looking at the smooth, white snow on the ground below. The wind had sculpted unique shapes among the drifts. The trees drooped heavily with snow.

Her gaze shifted to the distant cove and its charming lighthouse. The lights were there again, but this time, she decided to keep watching instead of running for cover in her bed. She stood and watched.

There were two sets of lights. One blinked to the left of the cove and was swaying in a vertical up and down motion, while the other made back and forth trips, crossing in a straight line. The lights continued for some time before they finally went out. Constance was too tired and climbed straight into bed, pulling the heavy blanket over her shoulders. She couldn't lie to herself. The lights made her extremely uncomfortable.

I'm acting foolish. I shouldn't be afraid. I'm certain there is a rational explanation for the lights. Unfortunately, she couldn't push back the memory of the hooded figures on her trip through the foreboding stretch of forest. They'd appeared like specters on the snow-covered roadway and vanished back into the sparse woods. And Edward's angry warnings didn't help to settle her mind. She shivered at her belief that he had never come into her room through the door. *I know I didn't hear him knock or open the door.* Thoughts of Edward Gerard made her blood chill.

There was more rapaciousness in his antagonistic manner than in all of Roger's bold advances. *At least with Roger, I know what his desire is, while with Edward...*

She didn't want to think or imagine what Edward's goals might be. Constance finally felt herself drifting into sleep. She embraced the pleasant lassitude that went through her body, clearing her brain of fear and doubt. She burrowed down deeper into her pillow, snuggling in the warmth of the blanket. The dream formed slowly. There was no pushing it back.

Snow everywhere! Great mounds of white brilliance. The sight of it made her shiver involuntarily. Just beyond the snow towered a large mansion, as grey as the swollen skies above. Everything appeared vaguely familiar, yet in the haze of sleep, Constance could not identify any part of it with certainty.

The sea of grey clouds became thicker and turbulent and the wind rose, crying like a thing alive. And then it began to snow. Heavy curtains of the white stuff enveloped the land around her, including the large house. Just beyond, she could see that something broke the falling snow.

Constance moved slowly toward it and the closer she came the more she realized it was a headstone. The wind nearly knocking her over, she bent to read the name. Weather had all but obliterated the inscription but she could make out a name: Georgina Bethany Gerard. Who was she and why was she dreaming about a long dead Gerard?

A strong blast of icy wind nearly pushed her back but she read the dates on the stone: Born 1792, Died 1792.

The snow swirled around her ankles. Constance wanted to run away, to wake up and be back in her warm room, but she couldn't. She literally could not move.

Suddenly, the snow began to lift up above the grave. Constance jumped back, realizing she could move again. She uttered a cry as a beautiful pale woman rose from the grave. She was shimmering and her naked body was as white as the snow upon the ground. The pale apparition set glittering green eyes on Constance and held out a hand.

And just as quickly, she was gone. Constance scanned the white landscape around her, but she was alone, until she spotted a dark figure standing behind the headstone a distance away. The bulky figure stood deathly still and seemed to be wearing a large coat and hat. Was it a man?

"Oh, my God!" Constance screamed and bolted straight up in bed. She was covered in perspiration. The heavy beating of her heart thundered in her ears.

Her room was nearly dark, only the low glow of burning embers from the fireplace cast a light. She left her bed and quickly lit several new candles. Slipping on her robe, she went to the door and sprang the bolt. Too frightened to return to bed and equally terrified to advance into the darkened corridor, she stood motionless.

Constance wanted to cry out into the dark, but knew that would wake no one. Her room was in the old wing and too far away from all the others.

Never have I had such a frightening dream. She wrapped her arms around herself. *If only I could speak about it to someone.* With discomfort, she turned and looked back into her room. *I cannot remain here all night. Dear Lord, what have I done wrong to be thrust into this unGodly place and situation?*

Leaving her door slightly ajar, she managed enough courage to walk back into her room and directly to the window. The sky was a deep black and filled with bright stars that appeared like sequins on black velvet. Constance could no longer see strange blinking or moving lights out in the distance.

As she stood looking out the window, Constance was finally able to calmly think about the disturbing dream. She chided herself for acting like a frightened child. She had overacted. But who was Georgina Gerard and why had Constance dreamed of herself standing in front of her headstone?

Feeling the chill, she turned to the warming fire. The friendly glow of the candles was reassuring. She rubbed her hands in front of the fire, straightened her shoulders and went to the door.

She knew there was no one in her room beside herself and to assure herself that there was no one lurking outside in the corridor, she stepped halfway out of the room and looked first toward the darkest part of the hall. It was totally black. Constance sighed in relief. Then she cast her gaze toward the head of the stairs, where the flame from a burning candelabrum illuminated that portion. Nothing was there.

Satisfied and relieved of doubt, she stepped back into her room. She started to close the door, then stopped. What if someone was hiding behind the curve of the wall next to the staircase?

What if I close the door and bolt it? No, I still won't feel safe. I must be certain.

Constance flung open the door and carefully made her way to the head of the staircase, fully prepared to take flight if need be. The candles in the candelabra were burning down and the light dimmer. She moved slowly, keeping her body hugged firmly against the wall. As she reached the head of the stairway, she paused before looking around the curve of the wall. Her heart was beating hard and it seemed like it echoed through the house. Resolutely, she sucked in her breath and circled around until she stood at the head of the stairs, looking down.

Startled, her hand flew to her lips as she saw a hooded figure slowly mounting the steps and heading her way.

The hooded phantoms on the road!

She drew back out of sight and pressed herself flat against the wall. The sound of creaking stair treads now drowned out the sound of her own frightened heart. She looked toward the open and waiting door of her room. Was it too far to make a run for it before being seen? To Constance, it appeared too great a distance to cross before the hooded figure reached the top of the stairway.

This has to be a dream. It can't be real! If I look again, this apparition will be gone and I will be in my bed.

Constance moved an inch forward. It was almost in front of her! The unwelcome guest carried a black candelabra that burned with seven black candles. Constance had to stifle a gasp as she noticed the ring on the hand carrying the satanic candles. *Could it be?*

He passed so close that she was able to glimpse his face. It was Edward. She froze as he turned her way, but he did not seem to see her. His expression was like a man in a trance. When she looked into his dark eyes, she saw the flicker of the candles' flames, and they reflected a void so deep that she felt herself being sucked into their blackness.

She cried out and looked away.

As if under some kind of spell, Edward kept walking slowly to the balcony and then crossed it.

When Constance could no longer see the light of his candles, she rushed back into her room, closed the door hard and bolted it. She soared into bed and dared not allow herself to dwell on what she had seen tonight.

She lay awake most of the night, waiting for the first rays of dawn's light, and only when the sky turned grey did she close her eyes and relinquish herself to sleep.

CHAPTER 9

"My dear Constance, what kept you?" Elizabeth Gerard questioned as Constance entered her room. "If there is one quality I admire most in those that I employ, it would be promptness. Perhaps you imagine that because I am unable to leave my bed, I would not care or notice the passage of time. Well, I will tell you, young lady, that I have very precious little time left and I expect you will respect my regrettable circumstances."

"I am truly sorry and I do apologize," Constance replied. "I spent a most distressing night and—" She thought of telling Elizabeth that she no longer wished to remain at Gerard House. She was even prepared to reveal to her all the strange things she had seen and experienced in the last couple of days, but she noticed an alarming change in Elizabeth that stopped her. She had closed her eyes and beads of perspiration appeared on her forehead. Her teeth clattered.

"The laudanum, please," she whispered. "Hurry."

Frantically, Constance searched for the medicine.

"Hurry."

"Where can I find it?"

"Up on the highboy." Elizabeth's words were followed by a loud gasp of pain.

Constance found the brown bottle and quickly administered a spoonful of the drug.

"Another," Elizabeth urged.

Constance hesitated.

Elizabeth pleaded. "I need another."

She gave it to her.

"Thank you," she whispered.

Standing by her bedside, Constance watched as the drug slowly took effect. The muscles in the older woman's face began to relax and her breathing became easier. Constance returned the bottle to the highboy and came back to Elizabeth's side. The old woman smiled up at her.

"Please forgive me for having been so hard on you," she said, reaching for Constance's hand. "My illness has made me a bit quick to anger."

Constance gave her hand a light squeeze. "I will be on time hereafter," she promised. "And now, if you are up to it, I can get you ready for the day." She looked at the only window in the room. "I believe the weather has cleared outside and we'll see a bit of sun today."

Elizabeth patted her hand. "I am certain we will get along very well together, my dear."

Constance spent the next several hours caring for Elizabeth. She'd watched a dear friend of her mother's care and tend to her ailing husband, so at least she'd be able to bring that knowledge to this job.

She washed her tenderly, brushed her hair to rid it of knots, changed the bedding and put her into a fresh gown. When she was finally done, it was nearly noon.

"Now, what shall I get you for lunch?"

The question surprised Elizabeth. "I really do not know what Marguerite has prepared or left for us today."

Constance explained that she would supervise the preparation of her food, and that she was to have whatever she wished for her meal.

Elizabeth sighed and shook her head slowly. "I'm afraid this pleasure has come when I can least enjoy it."

Perplexed, Constance looked at her.

"You must promise me to keep it a secret if I tell you."

"Of course, I will tell no one."

Elizabeth cast her eyes downward. "I can no longer take food, you know—" She looked up, appearing ashamed. "I can no longer swallow. The best I can manage are things like broths and oatmeal and such."

"But I can have some food mashed."

"And allow my sons and Catherine to see how I've nearly reverted to infancy again?" She shook her head. "I don't wish that."

Constance, touched by her pride, realized that Elizabeth Gerard was hastening her own end by refusing to consume proper nourishment.

"If I may be so bold, Mrs. Gerard—" Constance paused for a moment to consider if she should continue her thought. "Why bother to eat at all, then? What you are eating—or not eating—will cause starvation."

"Do not mock me, Miss Beechum."

"You know that I would not do so, Elizabeth, but if you hold to your pride, you will indeed hasten your death."

"I am already dead," the matron said in a defeated tone. She leaned back on her pillow. "All that is here is my heart and I only wait for that to stop beating."

"Then why not put an end to it with your own hand!" Constance blurted boldly.

The older woman looked at her sharply.

"You bait me, young woman?"

Constance smiled. "A mere nurse could not do that."

Elizabeth chuckled. "You will see to my food yourself?"

Constance nodded. "As long as I care for you." Just as soon as her words faded away, she realized she had already made the conscience decision about staying at Gerard House. She could not go, she thought, seeing how much Elizabeth Gerard really needed her. Her obligation was to Elizabeth and not to pampering her fears, which were meaningless compared to the pain and suffering Elizabeth faced.

"Then the devil with Edward and Roger."

Constance smiled again. "I will go to the kitchen and make sure I take care of it. And I'll have a private word with Marguerite as well."

After getting instructions on how to get to the kitchen, Constance found her way fairly easy. There was a narrow door near the stairs on the first floor just off the foyer. Once past the door, she found herself in one of the largest kitchens she had seen. Not that she was intimately involved with anything that had to do with cooking, but she and Lily had snuck through her household's large kitchen many a time in their quest for secret places to steal kisses. Lily. Constance pushed back the bittersweet memories and marveled at the kitchen before her.

It was a long, somewhat curious room, extending so long that Constance thought it surely had to take up a good quarter of the first floor. Red bricks lined one wall where there sat a huge open fire range, with large iron pots hanging from iron hooks in the ceiling. The shelves that lined the wall were filled with jars and pots, and hanging alongside those were also copper pots, iron pans and a glut of cooking utensils. Pots and bowls also sat atop several tables lining the opposite wall, which at one point was probably a bright yellow but appeared now to be a dirty ochre.

She went to a long pine table with apple green legs. It stretched through the center of the elongated room. That's when she caught movement behind her. The slim form of Marguerite stood behind her, with a mop cap that sat lopsided on her head. She held a tray of several loaves of bread in front of a crisp white apron.

"Oh, Miss, you gave me a start!" She put the tray down with a clatter on the large table and began to dust her apron off. "Are you the new nurse that will be looking after Mrs. Gerard?" Her bright green eyes sparkled in the dim kitchen that was lit by a single candle's glow.

"I'm Constance Beechum. I know we haven't been formally introduced." She held out her hand to Marguerite. "Yes, I will be taking care of Mrs. Gerard. And you must be Marguerite?"

Marguerite made sure to dust her hand more fiercely before offering it to Constance. "Yes, Miss, I'm Marguerite Maier." She presented a proper curtsy.

Constance smiled. "Oh, please, don't be so formal. Call me Constance, please. I'm hoping we can have more conversations on your days here. Everyone else has been less than welcoming, I'm afraid."

Marguerite looked at her, unsure what was required of her. "Oh, I don't know Miss—"

"Constance, please. Remember?"

Marguerite smiled shyly. "Thank you, Constance. Frankly speaking, they keep me very busy, but if you come down to the kitchen when I'm here, we can talk and share women stuff."

Constance offered her a wide smile. "That will work out perfect, because that's why I was down here in the kitchen. I will be preparing Mrs. Gerard's food starting today. Please leave me her portion and I will take care of preparing her tray."

The maid nodded. "Oh, yes, Miss—Constance, I mean. There will be no problem from me with that." She shook her head and leaned in closer to Constance. "It's a shame what they ask me to feed poor Mrs. Gerard. I wouldn't feed that food to my dogs."

Constance felt pained for Mrs. Gerard. But things were going to change now that she was nurse.

"I think we're going to get along splendidly, Marguerite. Now, if you will get me a pot of hot water, salt, pepper and a piece of that chicken breast, we'll get to work."

The next few days passed pleasantly. Constance began to learn her patient's moods and anticipated most of them. She'd learned she could do the job quite well. And her small victory over Elizabeth's food seemed to have enormous and beneficial benefits. Mrs. Gerard gained more color and had far more energy than before.

She saw very little of Roger and even less of Edward and Catherine. When she did see them, Roger was always cordial and effervescent while Edward scarcely acknowledged her. Catherine eyed her like a cat pacing a mouse.

She worked hard during the day, which thankfully made sleep at night easy. There were no more lights out in the cove and the unpleasant dreams had disappeared.

The only difficult thing now was having to witness Elizabeth go through agonizing seizures with pain so enormous that they seemed to flow from the frail and dying woman's body to her own. Constance broke down in tears several times. And sometimes, when attempting to administer the laudanum, her hands trembled so much that the liquid dribbled down Elizabeth's chin.

She looked at Constance and whispered through her torment of pain. "It is good to know someone really cares about me, even if that person is not of my blood." Her voice was filled with sadness.

She quickly administered her medicine. Afterwards, Constance had to move away from the bedside and stood by the window with her back to Elizabeth.

"Do not pity me, my dear. It is more than I can bear."

Constance wiped her tears with a handkerchief. "I would pity any man or woman who had to suffer as you are."

"The doctors have said it will get worse," Elizabeth said remorsefully.

Constance came back to stand by her bedside. "You are one of the bravest women I have met," she said, as she wiped the perspiration from her brow. "Far braver than even a man who makes his way on a battlefield."

Elizabeth managed a smile. "I am at least thankful for you. I'm afraid my marriage was one with initial euphoria but future disappointment."

Constance, happy that the woman felt good enough to want to talk, encouraged her. "I suppose all marriages come with their regrets, as does life."

Elizabeth nodded and her eyes glazed over as she stared into space. "And not only my own regrets for my mistakes but I suffer the regrets of the actions of my sons as well, although I've done what I could to make the most grievous of all their sins right. Although Edward likes to blame Roger for being an irresponsible cad, it was he who committed the greatest transgression."

Constance thought Elizabeth might be lapsing into delusions, but she wanted to continue listening to what her patron had to say.

"I certainly would not want my patients, or anyone else for that matter, clearing up the errors and mistakes I make along the way."

Elizabeth had a strange, far away smile on her pale lips. "Oh, but I've had the best time with the most delicious secret kept in the Gerard family. I've had to fool Edward and Catherine, and everyone in between, into making a great wrong right."

Constance was getting somewhat confused with her ramblings, yet she was curious if the feeble woman was about to reveal the great secret of the Gerard family treasure—the one that Edward and Roger were so keen to get their hands on."

She willfully edged her on. "Is there a secret in the Gerard family?"

"Oh, indeed there is! A living, breathing secret. Of course, Edward and Roger—and yes, Catherine too—are only interested in the Gerard treasure. Money and jewels are not treasure. Precious life is what constitutes a real treasure. A life Edward threw away."

Constance was certain now that Elizabeth had lost control of her thoughts and that she was now speaking in riddles. Of course, she didn't expect the Gerard matriarch to reveal any of the Gerard's secrets to her, a total stranger.

"You understand, my dear," Elizabeth continued, "that I harbor the biggest secret of all. It is a secret to a treasure neither Edward, Catherine nor Roger even suspect exists." She stopped and grimaced. Constance wondered if the pain was back. She offered her hand and smiled.

"I suspect that my dear sons are going to be quite in shock when I'm gone and the secret is finally revealed."

Constance heaved a sigh. She really didn't know if the older woman was of her right mind or not.

Elizabeth squeezed her hand. "I apologize if I have burdened you with my own ramblings, but I did not expect you to weep for me. I'm afraid I took advantage of your pity. And now, I would appreciate some tea."

Constance rose from her chair. She thought that she was probably sending her away so that she might be free of her dark mood.

"I shall return quickly with the tea."

"No doubt, I shall be here waiting." Elizabeth turned her head and looked away.

Though she had left more than half of her lunch on her plate, Elizabeth grinned widely at Constance. "Oh, it has been so long since I could say I enjoyed my food. How ever did you manage to get such a fine—" She paused, searching for the proper words, then she pointed a finger at Nurse Constance. "No matter what you say, I won't believe it. There can only be one explanation."

"And that would be?" Constance asked, delighted she appreciated her efforts in the kitchen.

"Witchcraft, my dear young woman. That surely has to be it."

"And if so, do you object?" Constance raised her eyebrows in jest.

Elizabeth stared at her. "You are a lovely young woman. I gather you have your share of handsome young men at your beck and call. Why have you not married?"

Constance blushed.

"Did my comment offend you?"

She smiled at her. Of course, she could not explain that she most certainly did have more than her share of men calling for her. She could not reveal that she had rebuffed them all because she had wanted only Lily. Lily with the soft, dark tresses, heaving bosom and coy brown eyes. Lily, who had toyed with her and then broken her heart.

"You did not offend me, Elizabeth." She lifted the food tray. "After I return the tray to the kitchen, I shall be back with your tea."

"Do you play chess, Constance?"

"I'm afraid you will have to teach me."

"Then I shall, and I shall trounce you."

"Why, Elizabeth!" Constance exclaimed as she left the room.

As she crossed the balcony, she found herself humming happily. She started down the long staircase and turned toward the kitchen.

"Miss Beechum."

Roger stood in the dining room doorway. "Do you always hum when you work?"

"I am sorry if I disturbed you," she said.

"Marguerite tells me you have taken to preparing mother's food."

Constance nodded and wished Marguerite hadn't been so quick to inform him.

"That is quite admirable." Roger grinned. "I hope that someday you might do the same for me."

Constance chose to ignore him.

"And how has my dear mother been treating you?"

"Better." She thought it wise to answer him and be done with the conversation.

"The ministrations of a beautiful and vibrant young woman and the touch of a gentle and caring hand is often stronger medicine than any concoction in a bottle a doctor can prescribe."

"If you will excuse me," Constance interrupted, wanting to escape. "But Elizabeth awaits me and I don't want to keep her waiting long."

"No doubt," Roger said, inching closer to her. "But I too have been waiting for you all these days."

"Do not be foolish," Constance snapped. "Your mother needs me."

"And I dare say, my dear lovely, I have my needs as well."

Constance was about to turn away when he grabbed her shoulders. She pushed him away by placing the tray between them.

"I must return to your mother. Release me at once."

"Promise me that we will meet tonight."

"I will not."

"Then I am afraid you force me to hold you this way until you agree."

Constance knew the only way to escape him was to agree. "All right, then," she said. "I shall meet you. Now, please, release me."

Roger grinned. "Now, that wasn't so difficult, was it?"

She felt his grip relax.

"At ten," Roger said. "Right here, at the bottom of the staircase."

"Of course."

"You will show up?"

"I will."

"Then go on to Mother's room." He turned around and disappeared into the dining room.

Constance had no intention of keeping her appointment with him.

I will not be forced into anything. Roger is much too spoiled.

She left the tray in the kitchen and a note for Marguerite to make sure they spoke tomorrow. The maid had to be more tight-lipped with what she told Roger, Edward or Catherine.

When she returned to Elizabeth's room, Edward was just leaving.

"She is asleep right now," he said.

Constance nodded and started to open the door.

"I must say, Miss Beechum, that your ministrations apparently have not improved my mother's condition in the past days."

It was an insult and it angered her. "I am not a miracle worker, Mr. Gerard, only a nurse."

"Then why continue prolonging her agony?" Edward asked.

"In God's name," Constance said, "Would you deny your own mother—"

"It is not in my power to deny her anything," Edward said and stalked away.

74

Constance squared her shoulders, took a deep breath, and allowed herself to relax before she entered the room. Elizabeth was resting comfortably, so she drew a chair close to the window and sat down to watch the passing seagulls. Tiring of watching the gulls in short time, she lifted the chair and was about to walk to the highboy where a stack of books beckoned. *Perhaps I will find one to interest me.*

A soft but determined knock at the door caused her to pause. She knew neither Roger, Edward nor Catherine would concern themselves with such etiquette. Would Marguerite? But it wasn't her day.

"Well, my dear, don't just stand there," Elizabeth said. "Go answer it."

"I thought you asleep."

The old woman smiled. "I was merely lying here resting my eyes."

The knock sounded again.

Constance went to the door and opened it. She found herself looking square in the face of the same gentleman they had picked up in the middle of the snow storm on the way to Castine. This time, there was no oversized hat or heavy coat to hide his extraordinary good looks. She could not find the words to clear her thoughts.

She took a step back, while the twinkling in the visitor's green eyes grew bright with surprise as well. He bowed slightly from the waist.

"Come in, come in," Elizabeth called from her bed. "I began to wonder why you have not paid me a visit until now."

The young man now smiled, never taking his gaze from Constance. His slender face was red from the icy cold, but Constance still marveled at how delicate he appeared for a gentleman. He wore loose, buff-colored breeches and high boots covered in tan suede. He removed his coat and threw it carelessly over one of his narrow shoulders. He held his coach hat in his hands.

"I must apologize, my dear Elizabeth," he said. "But the weather has been so terribly dreary and difficult. I could scarcely leave my house."

"Go to the fire and warm yourself, George, go on." Elizabeth pointed him toward the warm blazing fire. "You appear near frozen already."

George Kane moved to the fireplace and stretched his hands toward the popping flames. Once again, Constance noticed how slender and long his fingers were, and she admired the lovely black ring on his left hand once again.

"George, you are just in time to teach Miss Beechum to play chess," Elizabeth said.

"Oh?"

The older woman, more animated now than Constance had seen her before, only nodded.

"Permit me to introduce you to my nurse, Miss Beechum. She is also my new friend."

Constance curtsied and smiled.

"Constance, this fine gentleman is George Kane. He is our tenant renting the old lighthouse keeper's cottage by the cove."

Mr. Kane moved swiftly from the fireplace and took Constance's hand in his. Placing his full, soft lips to the back of it, his eyes ensnared hers.

"We had a most unusual introduction already, my dear Elizabeth, but this is much more preferred. I am charmed again, Miss Beechum."

"Thank you," she said. Her breath seemed to catch in her throat and she found the rhythm of her heart beat most irregular, making her breasts rise and fall.

What is wrong with you? No man has ever struck me so.

Mr. Kane let go of her hand, but his gaze still held her eyes intently.

"I thought I was surely hallucinating," he said, "when I walked up to the house and saw you at the window."

Constance, unexpectedly, felt her knees tremble at the sound of his mellow, young voice. How old was he? She found it still very light for a gentleman, but nonetheless, she could not deny her attraction to the sound.

"We did not get a chance to speak much in the carriage, but I wondered if you are from Castine or other parts of New England?"

He tossed his head back and laughed, and Constance noticed the long, dark ponytail trailing down his back. She thought him a dandy at first meeting, but his hairstyle was outdated.

"You could say I am Castine-born and raised." He turned away and with a graceful movement, flamboyantly slipped his cloak off. His tailcoat was a delicate green brocade, double breasted with a tan silk waistcoat touched off by a burgundy cravat.

"My dear Elizabeth, I would very much like to see how well you are able to teach Miss Beechum chess," he said.

"Do not doubt me," Elizabeth teased.

"I will wager that she will win."

"How sure are you?"

George Kane thought silently. "I play the winner."

"Done!"

The two shook hands.

"Now, dear Constance," Elizabeth said, "do you mind fetching the chess set on the highboy?"

As Constance turned and headed to the far side of the room, she had a most pleasant feeling that both Elizabeth and George exchanged knowing looks with each other. What secret were they sharing?

She set the mahogany chessboard down at the edge of the bed and following the instructions Elizabeth gave her, set the proper pieces in their place. All the while, she felt the heat rush to her cheeks as George Kane's gaze followed her every move. He continued to watch her as Elizabeth explained each chess piece, how it could move, and the purpose of the game.

As the game progressed slowly, Elizabeth asked George how the talk of war was going.

"Which war?"

"Why, between us and the Brits, of course," she answered as she moved one of her knights to take out one of Constance's bishops.

"Much as before," George answered, "though there is continued talk of skirmishes in Canada and American raiders doing damage to British shipping. Their ships continue to plunder our coast and kidnap our sailors."

Constance stole a glance as he was speaking. His face had hardened and the eyes darkened as he spoke. He was certainly passionate about how he felt. What stake did he have in the war if it became full blown? What exactly did he do for a living?

"I fear Madison is going to cave to the hawks," Elizabeth said, "and the Brits are foolish and arrogant enough to believe we are still their colony. They won't stop attacking and stealing our men." She stopped and looked at Constance. "What do you think of another war with England?"

She was surprised by the question. While the subject was good for idle conversation, she really had no interest in revealing her thoughts on the topic.

"Pardon me, Elizabeth, but I don't think much of those matters."

Elizabeth looked at her for a few seconds. "Perhaps you are right, but I feel that those who have sons who are taken off American ships to be pressed into His Majesty's Royal Navy would have strong feelings."

"I find it difficult to imagine myself in such a situation."

Elizabeth said nothing more to her, but continued speaking to George about the war for a short time. How could Constance allow Elizabeth or the Gerard's to know that indeed she was keenly interested in the war, politics and the fight to keep New England free. Things like marriage, keeping a home and a husband held no interest for her, yet it was what was expected of young women her age. If the Gerard's discovered her to be anything more than just a nurse, they would surely send her packing. She'd gotten comfortable at Gerard House and developed a fondness for Elizabeth. She didn't intend to ruin that.

The conversation began to take a different turn. Elizabeth asked George how his work on the lighthouse restoration was progressing.

"The persistent snow makes it difficult to get at the rocks, I'm afraid," George answered.

"Our Mr. Kane is restoring the Lighthouse Pointe lighthouse," she said.

"I found that some of the original rocks had been swept away by the ocean and carried into the cove, so that was a stroke of good luck to find them."

Constance looked up from the chessboard.

"Do you live near the cove, then?"

"Indeed, I do. You could say I live in it."

Should she ask about the strange lights? "Do you happen to see strange, blinking lights late at night?" she asked.

"Lights?" Elizabeth asked. "What lights?"

"Well, of course, I could not say," Constance said, "but I saw them the very night I arrived here and the following night as well. And I could have sworn I saw the masts of ships further out in the sea too."

"Oh, my," uttered Elizabeth, casting a look at George.

"I'd venture to say that it was most likely a coaster seeking refuge from the strong storms," George suggested.

"But the second night, the skies were clear and there was no storm," insisted Constance.

George stared at her for a second. "But how could you see the cove from this part of the house?"

"My room is in the old wing."

"My child," Elizabeth exclaimed, "why didn't you tell me that? What did they put you in the old wing?"

"I cannot say, but your son, Edward, thought it best."

"I'll have you moved immediately."

"Oh, no, please, I've gotten quite used to the room and rather like it."

"Are you certain?"

"Of course," she answered, looking at George. He was definitely disturbed by something. His eyes met hers and they burned with warmth as his face softened. He looked away.

After a few minutes of light-hearted play, Elizabeth cheerfully announced that she had Constance in checkmate.

"Apparently, you have beaten me in fair play."

"Well, you are a good player for your first time," she told her. "Good game."

"Why, thank you. I had a good teacher."

She smiled at her, relishing the change in Elizabeth's mood. She'd been positively beaming all afternoon. Had George Kane caused the good cheer?

"And now, Mr. Kane," Elizabeth said. "Are you ready to play this old woman?"

"I would be delighted, but I prefer, if you don't mind, to postpone our game until tomorrow. I should return to the cove and see if I can find any strange lights about."

The three laughed out loud.

"My dear George, I should like to plan a grand dinner and would like for you to please plan on attending, won't you?"

"It would be a pleasure, of course. I will look for the invitation." He turned his gaze upon Constance. "Now, I must get going," he said, taking his cloak and draping it around his shoulders. "It has been a real pleasure to meet you...again." He looked at Constance.

"Go ahead and accompany Mr. Kane downstairs, Constance," Elizabeth said, "I will be quite fine here."

"Oh, but I don't want to bother Miss Beechum."

"It wouldn't be a bother at all," Constance answered quickly, feeling herself blush again.

George nodded and held the door open for her, and after bidding Elizabeth a last farewell, he followed Constance out to the hallway. Halfway across the balcony, he paused and looked over at her.

"You know, there really is no need for you to travel all the way downstairs with me. However, this private moment does allow me to put your mind at ease regarding those strange lights," he said. "I am certain the lights were nothing more than one of our coasters."

She couldn't hold back a smile. "Well, Mr. Kane, I will remember your assurance the next time I spot them."

"And there is one other thing, Miss Beechum."

"Yes?"

"Elizabeth Gerard is a very special woman. I cannot relate in words what she means to me. Could you be extra mindful of her comfort and good health?"

His fondness and caring for Elizabeth warmed Constance's heart. "Of course, I will do my very best." Secretly, she was becoming more sure of her skills at care-taking. She had never thought she had it in her. This was certainly on-the-job training.

Unexpectedly, his hand reached up to her face, the tips of his fingers brushing against her cheek. His touch sent a hot fire through her. It confused her even further.

Then quickly, without another word, he walked away without looking back.

CHAPTER 10

That evening, despite the uplifting good cheer of the day, Elizabeth's pain became unendurable. Her suffering was so great that to prevent from crying like a schoolgirl, she bit her lip so hard that blood began to flow. She requested that Constance administer a higher dose of the laudanum.

"I cannot give you more, Elizabeth."

She continued to implore for more.

"Any more of the laudanum and it will cause your death." The painful memory of herself clinging to the bottle of the medicine in her apartment, before the fateful letter from her uncle arrived, inserted itself in her head.

"I am dying now, child."

Constance silently prayed that the drug would swiftly ease the terrible misery that made her patient plead for her own demise. She moved to the window and looked out at the serene moonlit landscape below. The white, shimmering snow was beautiful and the trees appeared as though they were covered in fine white lace.

How still and peaceful everything appeared. From the calm rhythm of Elizabeth's breathing, she knew that the drug had finally taken effect. She had now become addicted to the drug. The need for the peace it delivered from pain made her a prisoner to it.

Looking sadly at the sleeping woman, Constance couldn't help feeling helpless herself. She would never be able to restore Elizabeth Gerard's life.

She was interrupted by the unexpected entrance of Catherine, who walked over and glanced at Elizabeth.

"She's had a difficult time this night," Constance said, not looking at her.

Catherine ignored her, looking at the resting Elizabeth. "What a long way to die. Such a long time in suffering. Better that she go quickly than cause so much suffering amongst us. She has lived her life and now she should relinquish it to the living."

Constance's blood boiled. "If you must voice your insensitivities, I will ask you to express them somewhere else."

"But she is nothing to you, Miss Beechum. What is it to you whether she lives another day or dies tonight?"

"I don't have to explain that to you, and I do not feel inclined to continue this conversation."

Catherine Gerard turned her eyes away from Constance and went to stand beside the fireplace. "I thought I saw Mr. Kane leaving. Was he here earlier?"

"Indeed."

"And what is your opinion of him?"

"I found him beyond charming and extremely knowledgeable."

"I will make sure Edward knows of your appraisal and approval of Mr. Kane," Catherine said. "Our opinion is that there is something off with the man." She circled closer to Constance, her heavy sateen burgundy dress rustling along the floor. "I'm sure you must find it tiring to devote all of your time to the ill and infirm."

Was this woman trying to bait her into revealing that she'd had no prior professional nursing skills?

83

She shrugged. "I find it rewarding more times than not."

Catherine flashed a wicked smile, and the illumination from the dancing fireplace flames made her face appear like a demonic mask. "There are better ways to find pleasure, my dear. Work is not one of them."

"Most of us have to work, Mrs. Gerard, so that we may afford what we can."

"What a pity! It's so sad that you did not marry and now you are forced to work like the old maid that you are." She thrust one hand in the air.

Elizabeth moaned loudly.

"I must ask you to leave the room or bring your voice down. She could awaken at any moment," Constance insisted.

Catherine looked at Elizabeth.

"You should know that the laudanum does not hold the pain at bay for long," Constance warned, hoping that the woman would quickly disappear.

"I do know that. I cared for my mother-in-law before you got here."

Elizabeth moaned again.

Emboldened, Constance said, "I must ask you again to leave."

Catherine gave her a final, cold stare and dashed from the room in a huff.

Constance moved quickly to Elizabeth's bedside.

Elizabeth opened her eyes. "Who were you just talking to?"

Constance was surprised that she'd been so aware of someone else in the room.

"Catherine stopped by to inquire after your health."

Elizabeth closed her eyes and a slight smile creased her face. "That woman has no interest in my well-being, only what she can gain by my death," she whispered. "Do not trust what she utters from her lips."

"Perhaps you are too harsh in your judgment," Constance said, not wishing to offer her opinion.

"And you judge her not?" Elizabeth returned.

Constance preferred to change the subject. "May I bring you some water or tea?"

Elizabeth nodded. "My lips are parched. Yes, please. Won't you fetch me the water?"

Constance gently raised the older woman's head and held the glass for her as she slowly sipped from it. After resting Elizabeth's head back on the pillow, she promptly fell back to sleep.

Constance stayed by her side constantly. During the next two days, Elizabeth Gerard went from imminent death to an unexpected turn for the better.

But on the one morning when George Kane arrived for a game of chess, Constance had to inform him that Elizabeth's condition had worsened. That was before she got better. He became so concerned with Elizabeth's condition that Constance was once again touched by the bond the two shared with each other.

"I do not care what time of day or night you contact me. If Elizabeth passes or worsens further, I must be informed immediately." His green, almond shaped eyes watered as he gave his instructions.

Constance had assured him that she would personally make sure that he was contacted in a timely manner, and that seemed to reassure him.

That same afternoon, Elizabeth made an astonishing recovery. She seemed stronger, especially when she insisted on getting out of her bed. "Take me down to the dining room for my meals."

Constance was astounded by her surprise request.

"I am sick and tired of this bed and these four walls. I think I shall indeed die if I don't have a change of scenery."

Constance found Edward and Roger in the large sitting room, each with a glass of sherry. She approached them regarding their mother's wishes and requested help in getting her downstairs for dining.

"Absolutely not," Edward bellowed. "She is far too weak and frail, and she will not leave her room."

Roger was speechless. His gaze shifted between his brother and Constance.

"The change will do her a world of good," Constance insisted, surprised they both reacted so negatively.

Edward spoke stiffly. "So I am to assume this was your idea?"

"If neither of you fine gentlemen are up to the task of helping your mother downstairs to take lunch and dinner with us, I can always ask Mr. Kane and Marguerite for aid."

Edward pointed a long finger at her. "I warn you, Miss Beechum, if anything happens to my mother in your care, I will hold you completely responsible. I did not agree to your presence here, and I must remind you that I will make you pay dearly for my mother's death." His voice rose and octave.

Constance took his threat seriously and did not respond.

"I think that is enough," Roger finally said.

"I will ask you to keep your nose out of this, Roger."

Constance saw Edward's face turn a deep scarlet as he fumed in anger, while Roger merely cast his eyes downward as he took another sip of the sherry.

Constance was determined to grant Elizabeth's desire to leave her room, with or without aid from Edward or Roger.

CHAPTER 11

With Elizabeth resting comfortably, Constance decided to go and visit Mr. Kane and enlist his help in freeing the woman from her prison. She was certain he would heartily agree to assist her.

She left Elizabeth's room and proceeded to her own chamber in search of warmer clothes. Her scruffy old coat and hat and nearly threadbare gloves would have to do.

The air was clear and crisp, and the fresh snow like a white, soft blanket under her crunching boots. She so enjoyed making tracks on the snow and looking back at the markings behind her. She had never set foot outside of Gerard House since arriving, and was unfamiliar with the way to the old lighthouse keeper's cottage that Mr. Kane was renting. But Constance felt certain that by following the trail of tracks he had made when he visited early in the morning, she would find her way to him.

But even as she walked, the weather took a change for the worse. She glanced toward the Northwest. The sky was painted with hues of red, purple and blue, nearly overrunning the clear blue sky above her. And what had been a wisp of wind had turned into icy bursts blowing in from the Atlantic.

She thought she should hasten her step before bad weather caught her outside, unprotected.

As Constance approached the steep incline toward the rundown lighthouse, she caught sight of a small, dark-roofed house sitting just below a cluster of rocks at the base of the small lighthouse. The roar from the crashing surf below drowned out her thoughts.

She continued walking briskly until she was only yards from the house. Dark clouds suddenly swallowed the little sunlight that was left. The flicker and bounce of candlelight in the windows of the small cottage let Constance know that George Kane was home. The last thing she wished was to be stranded in a bad snow storm with nowhere to go.

Finally reaching a small patch of ground that was relatively snow free, Constance was able to stop and take a breath. Her legs felt like they could give way. The walk in the snow had been more strenuous than she thought.

There were three narrow, weathered wooden steps leading to a small porch. She noted the absence of chairs. There was a wide, four-pane window to the left of the plain, wooden door and the sudden urge to peek through the window before knocking overwhelmed her. Should she be so nosy to peer through a gentleman's window and invade his privacy?

Her first steps outside of Gerard House had invigorated her with a sense of adventure that she hadn't experienced in a long time.

Too long. She had to push back the memories of those passionate kisses in the dim candlelight of Lily's parlor room.

Constance shivered, and she wrapped her inadequate coat tighter around her as she approached the window cautiously. She certainly did not wish to come face to face with George Kane on the other side of the windowpane.

There were several single candles burning in pewter candlesticks scattered about the room. A fire was blazing in a small fireplace that was surrounded by red bricks with a narrow mantle. On the wall, over the mantle, were two rapiers.

88

On a round table in the center of the room, an oil lamp sat burning with a low, dying fire. Two large, rather worn wing chairs sat on both sides of the table, and across it—on the opposite end of the room, was a desk of dark wood that was piled high with books and papers. Constance could not tell what they were, even though her nose was pressed firmly against the glass. The walls were a deep green with oak wainscoting. The yellow pine floor was covered with small rugs. She saw no paintings or decorations on the walls. What an austere living environment for a gentleman such as George Kane. She'd gotten the impression he lived far better than this.

He was nowhere to be seen inside. *He must be in his private room.* She finally moved to the door and knocked, loud enough, she thought, for him to hear.

She waited a few more moments and when he did not come to the door, she knocked again, a bit louder this time. The cold began to creep into her bones and the wind intensified. Would he hear her over the shrieking wind?

Was Mr. Kane home? Worried that perhaps she'd been mistaken and indeed, the gentleman was not home, she went to the window again and looked. Nothing had changed and he was nowhere in sight.

What should she do? The skies had darkened so that it appeared to be near dusk instead of afternoon. Would the snow be far behind?

She'd noticed another window to the side of the house as she approached and decided to see if perhaps Mr. Kane was asleep in his private room and could not hear her knock. With the weather turning fierce, she had nowhere else to take shelter. Gerard House was too long a walk and she didn't think she could make it back before the worse of the storm took hold. What had she to lose?

Pulling her bonnet tighter around her head and turning up the collar of her coat around her neck, she began toward the right side of the house where the warm glow from a lighted candle in the window still gave her hope of finding Mr. Kane.

The ground was hard from the frost and she had to lean against the wind in order to prevent being pushed down on her backside.

She gave a sigh of relief that the window, if she stood on the tip of her toes, was at eye level. With her cold and stiff fingers, she gripped the window ledge and pushed herself up on her toes.

The few butterflies in her belly quickly turned into a roaring flock as she froze at the vision just beyond the window. George Kane stood naked in the bedroom, having just removed a most unusual corset. To her complete amazement, George Kane was a woman! The flickering glow of the candle and tiny fireplace cast an orange color over her pale, smooth skin. Two firm, perfectly shaped breasts held Constance spellbound.

She gulped down a scream, placed both her hands over her mouth, and slipped to the ground in shock and surprise. Her knees felt weak and she was having trouble breathing. She couldn't faint, not out here. She would die.

A flurry of emotions tugged at her. She now understood why she felt the strong attraction to Mr. Kane. Constance never reacted that way to men, no matter how effeminate they strutted about. The questions she was now determined to discover were very fascinating. Why was this woman masquerading as a man, and what connections did she have to Elizabeth Gerard?

Constance desperately wanted to look again at the beautiful woman inside the room, but she felt guilty. Who was she to steal another woman's private moment? But she could not control her curiosity and increasing attraction for this kindred spirit. The cold from the ground gathered up inside her and she began to shiver uncontrollably. But she had to take another look.

She gripped the window ledge again and peered inside. The room was empty! Where had the beautiful woman gone to?

Constance was suddenly grabbed from behind and a hand clamped over her mouth.

"I'm afraid I'll have to kill you now that you've discovered my little secret, Miss Beechum."

Constance struggled against the fierce hold of her assailant, striking out with her feet, but the other woman had pinned her arms tight and Constance couldn't move.

"Put me down now, whoever you are, or I will scream."

"I doubt anyone will come to your rescue. The Gerards would probably pay me to make sure you never return."

The voice of the woman who had been George Kane was not so threatening, but her grip remained tight as she briskly led Constance up the steps and into the cottage, closing the door behind her with a sturdy push from one strong leg. She released her once they were inside.

Constance glared at her in complete disbelief. She was dressed in a light coat, shirt and pantaloons with high boots. Her hair was loose, falling like black silk below her shoulders. Constance was surprised at herself for not feeling the least bit frightened, yet she was extremely infuriated at being caught and dragged inside like a common criminal.

"How dare you treat a lady thus?"

"Would you rather I denounce you to Edward Gerard for trespassing on my property and invading a gentleman's privacy by peering through my windows?" A crooked smile appeared then faded. "You know the Gerards are looking for any reason, even the slightest one, to send you packing, dear lady? I'd wager that would be reason enough."

Constance knew she was right, of course, but the most obvious and most pressing concern was to determine who this woman was and why was she was hiding her true identity? A horrifying thought crossed her mind. What if this woman was mad? Perhaps she was out to get revenge against the Gerards? Or was she after the Gerard's rumored treasure? For the first time, Constance felt a sudden chill of fear. But then why did this woman still captivate her?

"Are you really going to kill me?"

The woman facing her did not respond, but instead removed her coat and then held out a hand.

"I'm sure you're going to feel quite comfortable in here, Miss Beechum. Let me take your coat."

Constance, not yet sure why, followed her captor's instruction and took off her old coat and her bonnet too. The cottage inside was very warm and cozy. The situation had gotten beyond her control and at this point, she realized that she was completely at the mercy of whoever this stranger was before her.

"You need not threaten me regarding my visit to you. The way I see it, Miss or Madam, you are the one that will owe an explanation to the Gerard family. I will make sure I get one, too." Constance could not remove her gaze from the woman's open shirt and the peek of her breasts.

"I am not going to kill you, Miss Beechum," the woman said as she walked to her desk and motioned for Constance to take a seat in the wingchair.

"However, I may need to tie you and keep you in my dungeon for a brief time." She smiled, her green eyes twinkling with amusement.

Constance sat down, thankful to be inside and off her feet. They felt frozen. She could see through the window that a light sheet of snow was falling outside.

"The Lord protect me, I am now in your mercy since escape would now be impossible in this snowstorm."

The stranger glanced outside and back at her. Her face became serious.

"I cannot reveal my identity to you for several reasons, the most important being Elizabeth Gerard. It shall be she who should decide whether to trust you or not. I'm afraid, my dear Miss Beechum, that the answers must come from Elizabeth before they escape my lips."

Constance did not believe her, even though the intensity of the woman's eyes hinted at her sincerity.

92

"You expect me to believe that the Lady Elizabeth Gerard knows about you? That she is-privy to some ridiculous fantasy of yours and aiding in your disguise? For what purpose?"

"Ahh, dear woman, that is for Elizabeth to answer."

This bold stranger was more frustrating to Constance than she was threatening.

"Well, what shall I call you then?"

"George Kane, of course." She bowed slightly. "At your service."

"But you are not George Kane."

"To everyone in Castine and to the Gerard household, aside from Elizabeth, of course, that is exactly who I am."

Constance shook her head, and aggravation flushed her cheeks to scorching. She knew it wasn't just the heat from the blazing fireplace that was making her insides burn. She averted the other woman's gaze.

The woman came over to stand beside her. "You will need to stay here until the storm clears, Miss Beechum. Since this humble cottage has only one bedroom—mine—and being the gallant gentleman that I am—" she paused and smiled. "I will gladly offer my bed to you if you would like to get a bit of rest and privacy."

"I need nothing from you." That was a lie, of course. Constance did want something. She wanted to know everything about this woman with the fiery green eyes and ebony black hair. She could not sweep away the image of the fair, pale skin and beautiful breasts that had been revealed to her in secret. Would these images now replace those of Lily?

The other woman leaned down, and the scent of sweet clean soap incited Constance to inhale deeply.

"Tell me, Miss Beechum, what exactly were you doing outside my house in such God-forsaken weather? Why are you here?"

The woman's lips were so close that she could easily kiss them. Constance's heart was beating so furiously that she thought the other woman could surely hear it pounding. The fire that had been building up inside her exploded and she wanted to get up and run from the same feelings that had once ensnared her and led her into the arms of Lily.

"I see that you are speechless," the woman said, moving toward her desk where she pulled a bottle of sherry out of the desk drawer. "Why don't I pour you a drink to help you relax? You might want to rest after a sip."

Constance found her voice. "I came because Elizabeth has found enough strength to ask to come downstairs and escape her horrid room. She wishes to dine with her family. Both Edward and Roger declined to help me in bringing her down, so I threatened to come and get you."

Constance continued to stare at the flames bouncing in the fireplace.

"And I will gladly aid dear Elizabeth in whatever she wishes. Here, this will do you some good, in any case." Her hostess handed Constance the small glass of sherry.

Constance wanted to refuse it but she also wanted to swallow it up in one gulp. She took a small sip, watching the woman do the same. It tasted so warm and sweet to her lips that she drained the remainder of the golden drink.

She went to set the glass back on the table, but missed the edge entirely and watched in a daze as it hit the floor and shattered. When she looked up at the woman above her, she couldn't focus.

"You've put a drug in my drink." Constance attempted to get up but the room began to swim and the candlelight dimmed into darkness.

THE STORY OF CONSTANCE
AND GEORGINA

CHAPTER 12

Constance opened her eyes to a dim haze. She was finally able to focus and realized she was back in her own bedroom in Gerard House! She bolted up in bed, rubbed her eyes gently and shook her head of the fog that still lingered around the edges of her brain.

How had she gotten from the cottage back to her room in Gerard House? It had not been a dream, of that much she was certain. George Kane was not George Kane at all but a beautiful, haunting vixen. And a woman who had obviously given her some drug to put her to sleep.

What if she turned me in to the Gerards, inventing some sort of devious lie to protect her scandalous secret?

Constance had to find out what happened. She tried getting out of bed, but nearly toppled over, still feeling drained and dizzy. She steadied herself by grabbing the bed posts and inched her way to the window. It was nightfall. There was a nearly dead fire in her fireplace and fresh candles burned in two candleholders on her bedside table. How long had she been asleep?

She had to get to Elizabeth. Putting on her slippers, she noticed her boots neatly placed at the foot of the bed. The mud was still caked on the bottoms. If she'd doubted her experience at the cottage, the dirt encrusted boots confirmed the reality of the situation.

She managed to get dressed, slid a shawl over her shoulders and opened her door. The hallway was dark and silent. Where were the Gerards? Would she confront them only to find her bags packed and a trap waiting for her outside?

She couldn't leave Elizabeth now, especially without learning the truth about that woman in the cottage. She would never forgive herself if she left Elizabeth in danger, not only from her own family but from a possibly dangerous stranger in her midst.

She walked quietly, her candlestick held out to scan the darkness ahead of her. She had to see Elizabeth first thing. The house was very still. As she crossed the landing, she peered down below. There was only a flicker of light and silence. She didn't have time to wonder where the Gerards might be.

Constance crossed the walkway briskly, never looking back for anyone who might be following her. The most important thing was getting to Elizabeth.

At the door of her room, she hesitated before knocking lightly. What if Elizabeth was already asleep? From beyond the door, the woman replied weakly. "Come in."

The light in the room was faint. Constance saw that only one candle burned feebly, its tallow more than half gone. The bedchamber was stale, and the cinders in the fireplace scarcely burned.

Elizabeth managed a slight smile but her eyes glimmered with happiness. "I wondered if you had decided to flee Gerard House after all," she whispered.

"Has anyone come to tend to your needs?"

Constance was concerned about what might have transpired while she slept away the remainder of the day in a drug-induced coma. She spread an extra blanket over Elizabeth. The room was deeply chilled, like the air outside.

She couldn't suppress the guilt she felt over leaving Elizabeth at the mercy of her sons and Catherine. She felt incompetent and foolish for taking off on her own to find help, only to be deceived by someone she had previously trusted. Now, she would need to abandon her patient again to fetch kindling for the fireplace to heat the room.

"Catherine brought me dinner, but it wasn't as good as yours." Elizabeth was watching her intently. "She was none too happy with doing your job. She made it clear she was disappointed in you. I told her you'd probably overslept. I was forced to eat that horrible slop I accepted as food before you spoiled me."

Constance could not control her nervousness. "My most sincere apologies, Elizabeth." She tucked the blanket tightly beneath and around Elizabeth and placed her hand on her forehead to test her temperature. All the while, Elizabeth watched her closely.

"I'm not a mind reader, young lady, and I'm not running a fever. Are you going to tell me where you were? Are you ill? Have Edward and Roger done something foolish again?"

Constance could no longer put off the inevitable. The reason she had come to see her only trusted friend was to find out about the imposter formerly known as George Kane.

She let out a gentle sigh and pulled the chair up beside Elizabeth's bed. She idly brushed several loose strands of stray hair away from the older woman's eyes as she took just a moment to consider her next words.

"Yes, there is something terribly wrong, but it isn't any doing of your two sons or Catherine."

"Well, come now. The Good Lord isn't going to extend my time just for you to tell your story."

Constance didn't want to upset Elizabeth, fearing an onset of another painful episode when she advised the elderly woman of her recent discovery; but for their safety, she had to know about the stranger at Lighthouse Pointe cottage.

"Mrs. Gerard, how well do you really know George Kane?"

Within the silence that followed, Constance thought she heard a muffled gasp escape from Elizabeth's lips.

"I would trust him with my life. But why do you ask? Surely, that is not what brought you to my bedside at this unearthly hour." Her gaze remained steadily focused on Constance.

"Why do you place such a trust in him, if I may be so bold to ask? He is not your blood relation. He is, in fact, as much a stranger as I am."

"And yet have I not entrusted my life to you, dear child?"

Constance shook her head despondently, and the air around them was becoming oppressive. "I should just come to the point, because the secret I discovered today is threatening to burst from my insides."

Elizabeth said nothing, as she continued her quiet inspection of Constance with her unwavering gaze.

"I went to visit George Kane earlier today, since you had expressed a desire to take your supper in the dining hall. Your sons claimed it was a dangerous escapade, and they both refused to help me move you downstairs. I was certain Mr. Kane would offer his assistance." Constance paused, and the memory of the beautiful woman with sweeping black hair sucked all of her breath away, making it difficult to continue.

She swallowed hard, looking away from Elizabeth's patient scrutiny.

There was no easy way to divulge the truth. "Mrs. Gerard, George Kane is an imposter! He is not a male at all, but a woman masquerading as a man."

Elizabeth began to cough, and her eyes opened wide. Constance cursed herself for being so blunt and rushed out of her chair to reach for the glass of water on the bedside table. She helped Elizabeth take a couple of swallows.

The older woman finally waved her away after her coughing fit settled.

"I am so sorry, Elizabeth. I feared it would upset you. I shouldn't have said anything."

Elizabeth wiped off a dribble of water from her chin. "My goodness, Constance Beechum, if I had known you were going to turn out to be a detective, I would have dismissed you the first day we met."

Constance bowed her head. Would her job be over? Had she overstepped her privileges at Gerard House? When she looked back at Elizabeth, she was surprised to see a forgiving smile on her face.

"Tell me how you found this secret out, Constance. Don't leave any detail out."

Constance didn't know what to make of the situation. Was Elizabeth serious?

"I arrived at the cottage and knocked at the door, but after getting no response—and the weather seeming to turn for the worse—I decided to go around to the side of the cottage. That's when I peered inside one of the windows. I—" She paused again, not able to hold back the images of the slender, pale and very feminine figure of the imposter, George Kane.

"You saw her." Elizabeth finished the sentence.

There was a familiar fire burning in the older woman's eyes. The fire of deep love. Constance could feel the blood rushing to her head. The roaring sound in her ears was as furious as the pounding surf on the rocks. She was speechless.

Elizabeth laughed but it became more of a gurgle. She reached out a bony hand for Constance. "You probably think I've gone mad. Daft, to be sure. No doubt, you imagined I would be shocked into a fitful episode and need an extra dose of the draught."

Constance continued to stare at the elderly woman. "She took me inside the cottage and told me you knew everything about her, and that I should ask you for more information. She implied that you would have all the answers. I didn't believe her. I thought her to be a villain or thief, or someone intending to do you harm. I—" Constance couldn't continue. The woman on the bed was lying back on her pillow with her eyes closed.

As Constance pulled the blanket further up to cover Elizabeth, she opened her eyes and smiled at her nurse companion. "You, my dear Constance, have discovered the true secret of the Gerards. She is the Gerard treasure. The truest treasure of life."

Was Elizabeth Gerard delusional? Had she heard what Constance revealed? The woman did not appear to be in pain or feverish.

She pointed Constance toward her dresser. "Go to the bottom drawer. Open it and bring me the cedar box—and while you are there, in the top drawer you'll find paper, a quill and ink. Can you write?"

"My letter is tolerable." Constance moved to the other end of the room to the dresser.

"Good," said Elizabeth. "You will be writing a letter to your uncle after I reveal all to you."

Constance found a medium-sized box where Elizabeth said it was. The earthy scent of cedar wafted through the air. She brought the box and quill, a sheet of paper and the bottle of ink to the bedside table.

"The box is locked. The key is sewn into the bottom fabric of the high back chair. If you peel back the fabric, you will find it. Go on, now."

Constance was completely confused yet totally captivated with the excitement of the turn of events. She peeked beneath the flowery fabric of the chair, peeling back around the edges. Fingering inside gently, she located the metal key and yanked it loose. What an ingenious hiding place.

"Open the box. I lack the strength." Elizabeth may have been tired, but the excitement in her eyes shone like brilliant gems.

The small key turned the lock easily and inside, Constance found a document. Holding it up to the candles, she could see that it was a birth certificate.

"Can you read it?" Elizabeth was attempting to sit up.

Uncle Merriweather had taught his niece basic reading skills and the birth certificate was fairly basic. The handwriting was like chicken-scratch, but she could still make out names, dates and the name of Castine, Maine. The certificate had recorded the birth of a baby girl named Georgina Bethany Gerard, born the Eighteenth day of September, in the Year of Our Lord, Seventeen Eighty and Eight.

As Constance focused on the handwritten name on the birth certificate, the air in the room suddenly felt thin and the stillness was nearly deafening.

"Georgina Bethany Gerard." It was the name on the gravestone in her dream. A dream where she'd been lost in snow and blackness, and where a mysterious figure had beckoned to her from over a small headstone with the name: Georgina Bethany Gerard.

Constance wanted to speak but could not. She had questions that would not form on her tongue. She turned helplessly to Elizabeth with the certificate held limply in her hand.

Elizabeth pointed feebly to the paper. "That is the treasure Edward, Roger and Catherine know nothing about. It was a secret known only to myself and precious few others—people who have remained loyal to me. Until now."

Constance cleared her throat. "I...I had a dream several nights ago. It was dark and I was hopelessly lost in a fierce snowstorm. I thought I was here on the Gerard House grounds but I was not certain. Something drew me to a snow encrusted, small headstone. This name was engraved upon it."

Elizabeth nodded knowingly. "You foresaw what was to come, my dear. You saw only a piece of the puzzle. Now, you must see the entire picture."

Elizabeth patted the bed. "Come and sit with this dying woman. Whether you like it or not, your future is now tied to the Gerards."

Constance sat down but continued to study the certificate in her hand. Her gaze traveled to the bottom of the paper where there was a bold, red seal of wax. The name of Edward Gerard and Bethany Smythe were scribbled in a shaky hand. Both names appeared to have been written by the same hand. It did not appear to her that their actual signatures appeared anywhere on the document. She recognized only the wispy signature of Elizabeth Gerard and a public servant named Henry Adams.

She looked with confusion at Elizabeth. "Forgive me, but this is all too incredulous for belief. Are you asking me to believe the authenticity of this?" After her question, she thought how ridiculous she sounded. What purpose did Elizabeth Gerard have to have a fake birth certificate under lock and key?

Elizabeth coughed several times, clutching at her chest. Constance immediately reached for the laudanum on the table. The older woman waved her away.

"No, I have no need of that poison yet. Just water, please."

She drank carefully from the glass of water Constance held for her.

"I know this is all rather much for you to understand, Constance, but believe me when I say I have not lost my mind. Sit back down here and let me reveal the whole story of who my son Edward Gerard is, and who Georgina Gerard is, and why that document must never fall into my son's hands. Please, I must ask you to fold it back up and carefully replace it back into the box.

Constance did as Elizabeth wished, glancing briefly at the small window in the room. Night was still holding court outside. The sky was black without stars.

"I am not blind to any of my sons' shortcomings and faults, and I have always attempted to understand the warped reasons for their peccadilloes and tribulations they seek in their adult lives. However, Edward committed the sin that has no salvation—" Elizabeth paused but seemed eager to continue speaking. "He is dangerous, Constance. Watch your step with him."

"I can handle your son, Mrs. Gerard. I am not afraid." Although, she was beginning to wonder if she should not watch herself more carefully around Edward.

"But you should be. Bethany Smythe thought the same as you and made the foolish mistake that cost her her life...but not before gifting me with the beautiful child named Georgina—" She paused again, letting the words linger in the air like scented dust. "Georgina Bethany Gerard is living as George Kane and she is my grandchild."

Constance didn't know whether to cry in relief that George Kane was not some sort of monster in disguise out to do Elizabeth harm, or to scream in confusion. For the moment, she said nothing.

"I know you must be confused and frustrated, but forgive me. It takes this old woman some time to form her thoughts. My son Edward's marriage to Catherine was a tragic travesty. My husband, God rest his soul, arranged the marriage himself. For some reason that he deigned not to share with me, he became convinced that Catherine Mathers was going to be the only and best hope for Edward. I don't believe either one ever loved the other. Hugo, my husband, went out to sea and never returned. I was left with a household and a family to look after. Roger was rarely around. Edward grew tired of Catherine and began to have affairs, one of them with a beautiful kitchen scullery maid, Bethany Smythe."

While Edward Gerard was evidently more amorous and devious than Constance's initial appraisal, the fact that he carried on affairs with members of the Gerard House staff was not so notorious or monstrous. It happened in every large household where men of wealth and power always felt the women beneath them in station were candy for the picking.

Elizabeth was looking wistfully at her. "I know it doesn't sound so unusual, but most men won't commit murder to bury their infidelities. Only real monsters are capable of something so heinous.

"I believe my son Edward is one such monster. When Bethany didn't report for work one morning, I sent my son to check on her. The town folk mounted a search, hunting high and low for her, but she had simply disappeared. Edward suggested that she had left the area to live with relatives far away. I never believed that to be true.

"The next morning, the poor lass was found floating in the ocean below our cliffs when the tide came in. Nobody claimed her body, and apparently there was no one else who really cared how Bethany met her end. The investigation was swiftly dropped. But I cared about her dreadful demise, and I really believe my son had something to do with it."

Constance could hardly believe what Elizabeth had just told her. "How horrible! Surely, Edward did not kill her."

"His hands may not have been stained with her blood, but I'm sure he paid someone else—someone close and dear to our family—to do away with his daughter, Georgina. He could have done the same with Bethany."

"That cannot be!" Constance blurted out loud, refusing to believe a father could have his own child murdered.

Elizabeth nodded. "Unfortunately, the man he paid to dispose of little Georgina developed a conscience and had doubts about having the blood of an innocent on his hands. He came to me instead—" She paused, trying hard to catch her breath.

Fearing that Elizabeth was way past her bedtime and that the fatigue and excitement might be too much, Constance wondered if it was best that she leave Elizabeth so that she might get some rest and sleep. Yet, so many questions were still unanswered and unsettling in her mind. She knew she should not sacrifice the health of her ward just to satisfy her growing attraction and hunger to know more about Georgina Gerard. What a horrid life Georgina had led since her illegitimate birth!

Elizabeth interrupted her brooding thoughts. "I've lived a long and eventful life, young lady—and with the struggles, old age, and my impending death comes a wisdom that my Good Lord has seen fit to bestow upon me only at the end of my days. I know you have taken a liking for my Georgina, and she for you. You see, I've grown to know my grandchild like the back of my wrinkled, withered hand."

"Elizabeth, I—"

"No need to object, dear one, nor to defend your emotional attraction to my beloved granddaughter. I know what is in your heart and I know what drives my Georgina's heart as well." She stopped speaking and smiled weakly, but suddenly her emaciated body began to shake and her mouth grimaced with pain. She closed her eyes and motioned for Constance. "You must put away the box where you found it and hide the key as well. Get the laudanum, quickly."

Constance hastily stashed the cedar box in the dresser and tucked the key safely back into the hem of the chair. She would throw caution to the wind and give Elizabeth a larger dose of laudanum tonight. The older woman was shaking violently under the blanket.

She remained with Elizabeth until the draught calmed her sufficiently. But the strong-willed woman did not sleep. Even under the heavy sedation of the laudanum, she feebly motioned for Constance's attention.

"Before my body and my mind are whisked into blissful sleep, you must write a letter to your Uncle Merriweather."

Constance placed the sheet of paper in front of her, and took the quill in hand. "I am ready." She waited with anticipation and some trepidation, for she had no inkling of what Elizabeth wanted to convey to her uncle.

"Dear William, my honorable confidante. Through our long years of association and friendship, you have done me no greater service than to provide me with your wonderful niece, Miss Constance Beechum, as my attentive nurse. Her care has not only been a blessing to my soul and spirit, but my walk toward inevitable death has been brightened and made more bearable by her presence and capable hands. Her arrival will not delay my passing, but my transition will be far more comfortable and acceptable."

Constance could feel her cheeks blush. She was deeply humbled by the words of her mistress. She felt tears gathering but dared not cry for fear Elizabeth might consider her foolish.

"You have stopped writing and I cannot hold sleep at bay much longer," Elizabeth said.

"It is difficult to write when another is praising me so highly. I am not deserving of such high acclaim."

"What I've decreed is nothing but the truth."

"You are too kind," Constance replied softly.

"Believe me when I say that if you had been unsatisfactory, I would have sent you packing the first day you appeared before me."

"Do not make my cheeks turn hotter than they are now."

"I tell you, young lady, I would not have hesitated to dismiss you and give Edward his due. Now, let us complete the letter before I die."

Constance finished transcribing the letter, and practically glowed with the peace of knowing that she was truly appreciated and blessed. Not only had she found a calling in her life and bonded with Elizabeth, but the butterflies that fluttered in her stomach each time she thought of Georgina Gerard had her guessing that she might perchance have discovered a woman worthy of her love.

Elizabeth read the letter with drowsy lids. "Excellent. Now, make sure the quill has enough ink and I will attempt to endorse my signature. And while you have quill and paper before you, why not write out dinner invitations? You write while I give you my plans. Make sure Marguerite distributes them to Edward, Roger, Catherine and don't forget my darling Georgina."

By the time Constance sealed the letter in an envelope, and addressed it to her uncle's law practice in New York,

Elizabeth had fallen into a much-needed sleep. Constance noticed that her patient's chest barely moved as her level of pain resisted each breath. She lit a fresh candle, made sure the fire in the hearth would last through the night, and left Elizabeth to her fitful rest.

As she walked back toward the far wing of the house, she could not contain the palpitations of her excited heart. There was no denying the reality that she would visit Georgina again, but this time, it would be different. She was now equipped with the truth and that felt safe.

She would have to face Edward, Roger and Catherine in the morning. As distasteful as that would surely be, she had to find out what, if anything, they suspected of her absence today. Had Georgina—who was desperate to keep her identity a secret—gone to them as the gentleman George Kane and revealed her disgraceful visit to his cabin?

Constance undressed, slipped into her nightshift, lit one fresh candle, and made sure there was enough wood in the fireplace to keep her warm throughout the night. As she snuggled beneath her blankets, she murmured a silent prayer for a peaceful sleep for Elizabeth, and one for herself that was free of haunting nightmares.

CHAPTER 13

The morning light was just barely peeking through her window when Constance awoke. Thankful that she'd spent an uneventful night, she washed her face and hands, changed into a fresh dress and threw her favorite shawl over her shoulders. Once she'd finished her morning meal, she had determined to visit Georgina at the lighthouse cottage. She was hoping for a fresh start with Georgina Gerard. Besides, there were still more questions that Elizabeth had not answered.

Both Edward and Roger were seated at the dining room table. *Where was Catherine?*

Edward eyed her disdainfully when she entered the room, while Roger nearly tripped over himself to help her settle at the table.

"I was certain you had taken a vow to my mother that you would never leave her room again until her time to depart us all has arrived."

"Well, you should thank your mother for encouraging me to spend more time away with others."

She felt she could breathe a sigh of relief. It was apparent that neither Edward nor Roger had spoken to Georgina. This emboldened Constance.

"I was up late with Elizabeth writing a letter to my uncle—thanking him for my service and relaying that I am to stay here at Gerard House."

"You lie," Edward exclaimed. "My mother has been unable to write for many months."

"I am not lying," she said. "Your mother dictated and I set the words to paper."

"Ahh, so that was the letter I noticed on the foyer table earlier," Roger said.

"Indeed. I placed it there last night before retiring."

"I saw no such letter," Edward bellowed. "And my mother has not mentioned your staying. She must have been under the influence of the laudanum."

"I assure you, she was quite lucid."

They were interrupted by Marguerite, who set a large china tureen filled to brimming with soup in the center of the table. Constance, knowing how hard Marguerite worked on the days she was there, offered to serve both Edward and Roger herself. She winked at the maid as she took the ladle from her hands.

"I can serve myself quite adequately," Edward snapped.

"I would be delighted if you could serve me," Roger said with an approving smile, handing her his soup bowl.

Marguerite bowed and said, "Thank you, Miss," as she backed out of the room and disappeared through the door into the kitchen.

Constance eyed the amount of food set on the table throughout the meal. Since her arrival, the frugal amounts afforded to her and provided for Elizabeth, were meager. She was mildly shocked that Roger, Edward and Catherine ate so well by contrast. After the soup, Marguerite brought in a platter piled high with generous slices of ham, beef and fowl. A large tin filled with a vast assortment of breads, jams and fruits sat on the other end of the table. What could possibly be on the menu for lunch and dinner?

110

While Edward busied himself with an over-abundance of food, Roger spent his mealtime casting guileless, provocative and flirtatious looks her way. But he said nothing.

Constance grew weary of the unnerving silence which was wholly-magnified by the sound of Edward's smacking lips.

To end the tedium, she thought to address Edward directly, in hopes of stirring a discussion. "In conversation with your mother, she made a brief mention that you had traveled to England, and that you spent several years abroad."

He stopped eating and set a small chicken breast on his plate. "And what else did you two gossip about?"

"She said you traveled for Gerard business matters."

"Too bad he doesn't have much business sense." Roger laughed sarcastically.

"Did you visit many interesting places and see many interesting things?"

Edward continued to chew on his chicken, looking away from her. "You are attempting to garner favor with me, Miss Beechum," he said brusquely, between bites. "It won't work."

Constance eyed Roger, who only shrugged his shoulders.

"I thought that you might have spent some time in a church or monastery during your visit to England," she persisted.

Roger burst into loud laughter. "Now that is the wildest and most silly assumption I've ever heard about my brother!"

Constance didn't appreciate being treated in such a flippant manner. She had her reasons for the questions. She ignored Roger and bravely confronted Edward again. "I only inquired because of the robe I saw you wearing."

Edward stopped eating and placed both his hands on the table.

"A robe?" Roger asked, finally indicating some interest.

She smiled broadly. "Yes, the type that monks are known to wear—with a hood."

Roger cast a questioning look at his brother. "Why, Brother, you don't own any such garment, do you?"

"She is lying!"

"I have nothing to gain by—"

Edward sneered, "Why do I doubt that?"

"I saw you in a robe and that is the Lord's truth!" Constance persisted with a conviction that equaled that of Edward's denial. "I remember the night well. It was only a few nights after my arrival here. I was standing in the shadows of the hallway and you were coming up the stairs. You carried in your hand a seven candle candelabra with black candles."

"Black candles?" Roger's eyebrows arched.

"She is a liar!"

"Well, I want to hear what else Miss Beechum saw," Roger invited. He was obviously completely enthralled with her story.

Constance laughed self-consciously. "That was all, I'm afraid. I ran to my room, locked the door, and hid under the covers."

Edward objected to Roger's request. "Can you not see how absurd her fabricated tale is?"

He fixed his eyes on Constance. "You expect us to believe that we—you and I—were so close that we passed each other in the hallway, yet I did not see you." He shook his head with a self-satisfied smirk. "Pure rubbish!"

"You were indeed so close to me, Mr. Gerard, that you even looked at me straight in the face...but if I may be so bold to speak further truth, you appeared to be intoxicated by too much drink."

"Oh, no," Roger said with great seriousness. "My brother does not touch anything but the occasional sherry. Is that not so, Edward?"

"I will not sit here and be subjected to this woman's lies!"

"We need not get so testy," Roger said, seeing the redness of anger building in his brother's face. "There is no need for all of this hostility."

Edward glared at his brother, who had set his gaze on Constance as he continued his speech. "We know how uptight you've been over Mother's state. You cannot hold poor Miss Beechum responsible if our precious mother is taking her sweet time to say goodbye to the world before she enjoys the next."

"How could you be so—" Constance began, but she was interrupted by the younger brother's continued discourse.

Roger turned his attention back to his agitated brother. "Nor is it Edward's fault for desiring our mother to expedite her death. After all, he feels he is to inherit this stately house and all the Gerard riches."

Constance stood up immediately. "This conversation is not only insufferable, but unGodly," she said reproachfully. "I will not sit here one moment longer and be privy to it!"

She was nearly to the bottom of the staircase when she felt a strong hand grab her arm tightly and she squealed as she was roughly spun around. Roger stood facing her.

"I do not wish to speak to you any further, you loud-mouthed bore!"

"But I wish to speak with you."

"I can think of no worthwhile conversation with you, Sir. Release me now so that I may return to my room to refresh before tending to your mother."

"Please, do not go until you promise to meet with me," he practically begged.

Constance looked at him, shaking her head. "I could never imagine you being so callous about your own mother."

He put one hand gently over her mouth. "That was purely for my brother's benefit."

"But you have voiced the same opinions before," she accused.

"Agree to meet me, dear Miss Beechum, and I will explain my actions to your satisfaction," he said. "I do not wish you to think me a heartless son who wishes to gain from his mother's death. Say you will meet me, please."

"I will give it some thought," she tersely replied.

He released her and apologized.

Constance turned and rushed up the stairs without looking back, yet knowing with certainty that Roger still stood watching her hurried steps. She cared not what he wanted or whether he was a monster like his brother.

The only thing that mattered now was to get back to Georgina—Georgina and that enticing, warm cottage. She could already smell the beguiling scent of her porcelain skin.

When he made sure Constance had disappeared into the upstairs hallway, Roger turned and headed slowly back to the dining room and his sullen brother. While he thoroughly enjoyed watching her as she mounted the stairs, he paused for a more pressing reason. Were her accusations about Edward true? He was convinced the woman was as honest as a wench could be. He was well-read enough to know what black candles were used for and why. If his brother was involved in what he feared, he may have to be very generous with whatever treasure might be willed to him. For a tidy sum, he could keep secrets. But first, he had to be absolutely certain about his suspicions. Roger smiled smugly.

He entered the dining room and took his seat quietly.

"You had to chase that bitch, didn't you?" Edward growled.

"Oh, come now," Roger chided. "The woman was upset, and I am a gentleman. I had to offer her my shoulder."

"You flatter yourself still. You will never change," Edward said.

"I do not wish to continue arguing." Roger reached for the wine and poured himself a full glass.

Edward pointed a finger at him. "Sometimes I am convinced your brain cannot think beyond the size of the mattress where you bed a wench."

Roger ignored him and took a long drink of the wine before looking at his brother.

"And I have wondered about your lack of such a hedonistic place." He paused, then added, "We all have animal tendencies and desires."

"And just what does that remark imply?"

Roger shrugged. "It is quite obvious that Catherine does nothing for you, and you are so old that the fires of passion have been snuffed—"

"You go too far, brother," Edward warned.

"Perhaps." Roger ignored Edward's steely gaze. "You really have become a monk, as Miss Beechum accuses."

"How dare you!" Edward pushed away from the table. "You will regret this," he said, nearly choking with anger.

"Don't take my words so seriously." Roger laughed self-indulgently. "It still amazes me how you fail to recognize that winning the good graces of mother's nurse could be to your advantage."

"I care not. I will have her out of this house."

"Edward, that lovely flower of womanhood could be persuaded, with a good bedding and sweet words, to sway our mother to do just about anything with her Will."

Edward shook his head and sneered. "I will need no such tool." Again, he pointed a finger at his brother. "You are the one who needs a grappling hook to pull yourself closer to mother's good graces and a piece of that Will. It is you who are attempting to do just that with that miserable wench. It will not work. I am to be the next Master of Gerard House."

"Don't be so smug and sure of yourself. Many an old woman close to death's door has altered her Will," Roger replied calmly.

"Mother is not such a fool as to not see you for what you are; An irresponsible womanizer and vagabond!"

"I wonder, Edward, who between us is the worst devil?" Roger looked his brother straight in the eyes. "That is a subject I would like to take up at a more opportune time."

CHAPTER 14

Constance knew she had to be as expedient as possible. She did not want to get back too terribly late, plus she had to get away from the house while Roger and Edward were still at the dining table and Catherine occupied elsewhere.

And where did Catherine spend her time? What did she busy herself with?

She made sure Elizabeth was taken care of and informed her that she had to escape to see Georgina. Then she bundled up in her old coat, bonnet and scarf and sneaked her way out of Gerard House.

Despite the risk involved, her fluttering heart drove her inexplicably to Georgina Gerard. And the hunger for answers. Elizabeth was old and frail. There had been much she'd left unanswered. Constance was certain the mysterious daughter of Edward Gerard would reveal the answers.

Mercifully, the sky was dark and grey, but there had been a whole day without snow. Although it was bitterly cold, the walk to the cottage was easier than the previous trek. The wind still swirled in the dark, and stained leaves twirled about her as she walked.

As she rounded the old, crumbling side wall of Gerard House, Constance thought she heard footsteps crunching in the snow behind her. She whirled around but saw no one and the strong wind was sifting the snow about. If someone had been trailing her, the footsteps would be covered over. Even so, where could they hide? Behind the old side wall of the house?

Pushing it aside as part of her nervous imagination, Constance continued the path up to the old Lighthouse Pointe cottage. The anticipation of seeing Georgina again made her tremble. Was she being foolish again like she had been with Lily? Georgina had given her no indication that she too was feeling the same kind of attraction that was now consuming Constance.

When she finally reached the foot of the cottage, Constance took another glance behind her. Only wisps of wind-blown snow swirled the landscape.

Suddenly, she began to wonder if she'd done the right thing by coming here. What if her absence was noticed again by Edward? Elizabeth would surely offer up a good explanation to him, but his raging mind would find suspicion in whatever excuse his mother offered for why her nurse was not at Gerard House presently taking care of him.

She had to be quick with Georgina and rush back to Gerard House in haste.

Immediately, Constance noticed that curtains had been drawn over the front window. There was a slight opening in the center where the curtains did not meet, but that only allowed Constance the view of the very middle of the room and the fireplace. She had no way of sneaking a peek to see if the woman with the fiery green eyes was sitting at her desk to the far left wall, or even if she was home at all. There was no time to waste.

She knocked firmly on the weathered door. The door opened wide and Georgina Gerard stood staring in surprise, but she was dressed as George Kane. It almost gave Constance

117

a quiet delight to see the shock in the other woman's face. Though fully attired in waistcoat, cravat, buff colored pantaloons and boots, Constance no longer saw an effeminate man but the vision of a shapely and beautiful woman dressed for a masquerade.

"Will you be a gentleman and invite a lady inside, or are you going to continue standing staring at me while I freeze to death?" Constance smiled sweetly.

Georgina swung the door open, bowed and waved her inside with a flourish. Before closing the door, she poked her head outside and looked along the path where Constance had traveled.

"Don't worry," Constance said. "I haven't brought the Gerard clan upon you." She began to untie her woolen bonnet and her coat. The fire in the fireplace was low, but warmed the room enough. She handed Georgina her coat and bonnet, feeling more empowered and comfortable in her second visit to the cottage. She was now equipped with knowledge that had been forbidden to her before.

"If you don't feel the need to attempt to poison me again, I will take a sip of sherry, please."

Constance watched as a still dumbfounded Georgina placed her coat and bonnet on the small table and walked to her desk. It was still littered with large pieces of paper that appeared to Constance to be maps. Lying atop the clutter of maps was a compass, protractor and sextant. She knew those to be tools of a map-maker or sailor. What was Georgina Gerard doing with such things?

Georgina poured two glasses of sherry and handed one to Constance, who still stood by the fireplace.

"And what, may I ask, do I owe the dubious honor of your visit, Miss Beecham?" She brought the glass of sherry to her lips and eyed Constance. "Don't worry, my dear lady, I have not put a drop of questionable substance in your apéritif." Her lips curled in a slight smile.

"You would have no reason to distrust me at this point—" Constance paused. "Georgina."

Constance watched the flicker of both surprise and relief cross the other woman's face. She took a small sip of the amber-colored wine and let it slide slowly down her throat. The sweet alcohol pleasantly warmed her insides. She could feel its heat rising to her face and once again, she hoped her rosy cheeks would not embarrass her. Georgina took a big swallow and finished her sherry in one expert swallow. She stood closer to Constance and the warmth from her body was becoming almost too much for Constance to bear.

Georgina's black hair shimmered in the firelight and the reflection of dancing flames lit up her deep green eyes. Constance could feel fire rushing like molten lava up her body. Was it possible to become a human volcano?

"Then I am to assume you have spoken with my grandmother?" Georgina murmured, as she moved so close to her that Constance tried hard not to inhale the heady scent emanating from her. It was an intoxicating mix of alcohol from her warm breath against her neck, and the spicy-sweet fragrance from Georgina's hair and clothes. She took another sip of her sherry and lowered her gaze away from the intense eyes of the woman standing too close by.

"I pray you find it in your heart to place trust in me because, yes, Elizabeth did reveal the terrible truth regarding your mother and Edward...your father." She paused. "I am so sorry." Constance reached out to touch Georgina, but then pulled back her hand. "However, I'm afraid your grandmother left me with more questions than answers."

Georgina walked away and stared into the fireplace, keeping her back to Constance. "And you've come to me for those burning questions. Am I correct, Miss Beechum?"

Constance caught the very subtle pain in Georgina's words. It was not her intent to hurt Elizabeth's granddaughter. She wasn't here for that purpose. What she was beginning to question herself about was why, exactly, she found herself here at all. Why had she left Gerard House and sickly Elizabeth Gerard alone just to confront the beautiful woman before her? She did not think she wanted the answer to that question just yet.

"Perhaps I was rude and out of place when I called you by your first name, but now that I have done it, will you please call me Constance?"

Georgina turned to face her again, a charming smile curling the ends of her alluring mouth. "Very well, Miss Constance—"

"Constance, please."

Georgina eyed her steadily and offered a kindly nod.

"May I at least offer you a chair so that we may converse, Constance? I have a few moments that I can spare you and I would be a total cad if I did not hear you out."

She motioned with her hand to one of the high back chairs facing the small table in the middle of the room. Constance took a seat on the red velvet one, smoothing out her dress as she drained the final drop of sherry and placed the empty glass on the table.

"What type of work do you do that requires a compass and protractor? I never imagined restoring a lighthouse would require tools to navigate the waters."

Georgina took the chair opposite Constance and slung one booted leg over the armrest, gazing curiously at Constance. She leaned back in her chair.

"You amaze and perplex me, Constance. And you draw me in with your innocent airs, but your eyes betray something far deeper and more passionate."

The way Georgina's gaze traveled the length of her caused Constance to shift uneasily in her chair, an ineffectual attempt to still the roar of her pounding heart in her ears. The woman knew! Constance was convinced Georgina saw the fire that was burning in her eyes.

"Do not think I have not noticed that you have steered me away from my question pertaining to your work. Nevertheless, that isn't really why I'm here, and I do not have the luxury to engage in an extended visit because I cannot leave your grandmother to herself for long."

Georgina placed her hand on her chin and smiled. "I am at your beck and call, Constance. If there is anything I can do to help in your quest for answers, it will give me great pleasure." She flashed a wide smile.

Constance cleared her throat. Damn it. What was happening to her? Her thoughts had turned to mushy oatmeal and she wanted nothing more than to stay here with the captivating temptress who was still dressed in a man's uniform. How could she have allowed herself to fall into another emotional trap? These feelings had been bottled up after Lily Sinclair had ripped her heart out and trampled on it while it still laid beating upon the floor. Evidently, Constance had uncorked the same bottle again, this time quite willingly and perhaps recklessly.

Georgina unexpectedly reached out and took Constance's hand, holding it gently in her long, elegant fingers. She leaned toward her, searching her eyes for a sign of approval.

"You must surely understand now how much my grandmother means to me, and how much I appreciate what you have brought to her last days. I am in debt to you, Constance. Deeply in debt." Her voice was soft and very sincere.

Constance could not stop herself. She leaned in to meet Georgina's sweet, full lips and feel of the warmth seeping through her body as it erupted into a full blown fire.

Georgina did not resist the kiss, but instead, intensified it. She took hold of both of Constance's arms and held her tenderly as she returned the kiss in full.

It was Constance who broke it off and pulled away, searching the face of the beautiful woman across from her. She couldn't speak and had to tame her pulse as it raced beyond control. It had been like this with Lily. The fear of loss again threatened to erase the euphoria of her first kiss with

Georgina. Surely, this would not end like it had with Lily? Life would not be that unfair.

Georgina, noticing her withdrawal, studied her face intently, still holding on to her shoulders.

"Please forgive me, my dear Constance, if I acted like a brute and took advantage of you."

Constance studied the sincere green eyes and began to laugh hysterically. She tried to cover her uncontrollable hysterics with her open palm.

Georgina backed off and sat in her chair, a perplexed and wounded look on her face.

"Go ahead, then. I suppose I do deserve all of that for acting the way I did."

Constance put out her other hand in protest.

"Oh, no, Georgina, it isn't like that at all," she said between bursts of laughter. "It was I who acted out of place."

She finally stopped laughing and reached out for Georgina's hand. "It is so complicated, dear Georgina, and I promise I will explain it all to you one day." She was still burning hot and the flames in the fireplace only added fuel to her fire.

"Then tell me now, Constance, because I have been smitten by you since we met on the coach to Castine that snowy day." She had moved down on her knees to the floor, her hands now resting on Constance's lap. "I wish to know everything about you. I want nothing to stand in the way of our feelings for each other."

Constance inhaled deeply, letting out a slow breath. This was happening so quickly. And what exactly was happening? Georgina was right. There had been an inexplicable attraction—an instant intrigue—between them at their first meeting. But Georgina had been George Kane then, and Constance remembered her confusion at her interest in a man. She had to regain control of her emotions and at least attempt to retain a modicum of restraint.

"But when we met, you were a man."

122

"You knew, Constance. You simply either had your defenses in place or other things were on your mind. You cannot deny it. I beg you, do not put obstacles between us. We shall have enough of those as it stands."

She was right, of course. Lily Sinclair be damned. She was here all alone now, in a harrowing situation at best, and surrounded by people who wished her harm or even dead. In this cold, winter land surrounded by death and evil, she had found love.

Constance leaned over and kissed Georgina again, but only a quick kiss, as she searched her clear, green eyes.

"I must get back to your grandmother. I fear I have been away too long already." She brushed Georgina's silky smooth cheek. "Believe me when I say that I would prefer to remain here with you, my darling, but think of what the Gerards will say. They will accuse me of having a secret and illicit affair with George Kane and they'll stir up a scandal. That won't help us or your grandmother at all."

"Who cares of scandal out here? The Gerards are cut off from everyone in Castine, and not just by the snow. I thought you an enlightened woman. A woman not mindful of all the pompous etiquette stuffy society imposes upon us."

"I am all those things, my dear Georgina, and oh, if only you know how much I have lost because of those very rebellious attributes. I am unmarried and penniless. I was so desperate that I forced myself to take this job. I jumped at the opportunity afforded by my uncle. It was the job at Gerard House or suicide by poison."

She heard the words escape her lips and watched the reaction in Georgina's eyes. Her eyes widened in shock and she grabbed hold of Constance's hand, burying her head in her lap.

"You mustn't ever think of doing such a thing again."

She got up, pulling Constance up with her into a tight embrace.

"I will not desert you, Constance Beechum. I can promise nothing because these times are dangerous times, but my heart, once promised, is forever committed."

Constance remained silent, her teary eyes fixed on Georgina, as she tried to prevent from fainting with joy.

Georgina ran her fingers along Constance's lips. "You saw me, didn't you? Through the window."

Constance thought about the answer. Would Georgina resent her intrusive snooping? She only nodded, lowering her gaze.

Georgina lifted her chin up and kissed her, hard and deep. And then the sound from the window broke them apart.

Both of them looked toward the window where what sounded like footsteps interrupted them. Georgina immediately ran to the door and swung it open. Running outside, she looked toward the path but found nothing. No one was there. There was only the incessant pounding of the ocean below and the strong wind wrestling the trees. A slight dusting of snow had occurred at some point.

She motioned for Constance to stay inside until she made sure all was safe. She closed the door behind her and took hold of Constance's shoulders.

"You should go back. I could not see if there were extra tracks on the snow because even your tracks have disappeared beneath fresh snow." She gathered Constance's bonnet and coat and dressed her in them quickly.

"Georgina, you begin to distress me," Constance said as she tightened the string on her bonnet and buttoned her coat to the collar. "Do you believe someone was here, spying on us?"

Georgina led her to the door, smiled, and gently kissed her lips again. "There is no need to fear, my dearest, but it's best that you return to my grandmother with haste. We shall meet again, soon, I promise."

How could Constance feel any fear with Georgina Gerard as her rescuer? She was of formidable character. She was ready to walk out the door when she fingered Elizabeth's dinner invitation in her coat pocket.

"Oh, wait." She turned back and handed the invitation to Georgina. "Your grandmother has planned a grand dinner. She expects your presence." She gave Georgina a quick kiss.

She left the cottage and Georgina's warm embrace to face an unusually strong, biting wind that was blowing in from the sea.

The gale was so brutal and unpredictable that she entertained the thought that even the weather was somehow conspiring against her. Fierce squalls whipped the snow into violent little twisters as she struggled to travel the path back to Gerard House.

She finally caught sight of the crumbling wall adjoining the mansion. Walking through the snowy storm was more difficult than she had anticipated, and she quickly realized she was gasping for air. Every icy cold breath seemed to freeze her heaving lungs. She paused briefly to calm her herself before continuing toward her goal.

She could see portions of Gerard House. Not even a light shone through a window. It stood silently defiant against the buffeting winter elements.

I should continue going. She feared she might die so she wrapped the bonnet tighter around her face and covered her mouth with her scarf.

She was now only a few distant yards from the old wall and upon reaching it, she was suddenly buffeted by another strong gust of wind, which flung a heavy portion of snow over her head. She shielded her face against it, putting out both her hands. She paused until the drift subsided, then turned to proceed toward the welcoming warmth of the house. That was when she heard a sharp snap of gunfire. She felt the air beside her left ear tingle and a muffled thud hit the snow-covered ground directly behind her.

A gun shot! She felt her head to make sure she had not been hit. Jerking around to run, she stumbled and lost her balance in the snow. She clawed her way for a distance, wanting desperately to be away from the line of fire.

Constance managed to finally get up from the ground and ran the rest of the way back to the house. When she finally reached the front door, she turned toward the old crumbling wall. Even through the wind and swirling pockets of snow, she saw a dark figure standing at the top of an undamaged portion of the wall.

"Oh, dear God," she implored, "do not let me die out here!" She shut her eyes tight and when she was brave enough to open them, the figure was gone. "I know I wasn't imagining it. I know it was there."

Someone had shot at her. Someone wanted her dead and gone.

CHAPTER 15

Roger grew impatient for Constance to agree to meet with him. She'd put him off for the last time. His schemes would not be thwarted by some lovely wench. And if he could get her to bring down his brother, all the better. Things could take a turn for the better.

He admired his brilliant ability to scheme. He would have to alter his approach toward the wench and draw her into trusting him. He had no doubt he could accomplish that task. He'd always gotten what he wanted with women.

He hadn't been able to find Constance anywhere in the house, but he still hadn't checked the kitchen. He purposely avoided that room and decided to check her quarters once again.

A few minutes later he stood, exacerbated, in front of her door for a third time that day and knocked. He put his cheek to the door and listened intently for any sound from inside.

"Who is it?" she called out.

Success!

He hastily stepped backward into the hallway lest the aggravating wench should discover his inquisitive ear pasted to her entryway. He inhaled deeply and exhaled softly through pursed lips to calm his frayed nerves.

"Roger."

"What is it that you want?" Her voice sounded strained.

He leaned against the door frame and spoke softly. "I really must converse with you."

"I am exhausted and must shortly tend to your mother."

"Do not deny me. Please."

A moment later, the bolt slid open and Constance swung the door wide. He stepped inside quickly, hoping to get in before she changed her mind and closed the door on him. The dark room was lit only by the fire burning at the hearth.

"Now, what is your urgency?" Constance stood with her simple dress and shawl drawn tightly around her shoulders, and her arms protectively crossed at her bosom. She stared defiantly at him.

"I wish to speak to you regarding my brother," he said, casting his eyes upon the crumpled, wet dress that rested barely peeking in a puddle beneath her bed.

Constance saw where his attention was affixed and shrewdly shifted to block his view of the dress she had just removed in haste.

"There is no need to continue our hostilities," he said gently. "I feel I need to ask your forgiveness again for the rude manner I have thus far displayed."

"You've already apologized enough," she said. Constance took a candle and bent down to the fireplace to light it.

"Will you allow me, Miss Beechum?" Roger politely took the candle from her hand. Once it was burning, he set it down on her dresser. "Now, about those hooded figures and my brother Edward. You say you saw—"

"I encountered your brother in the hall one of the first nights I resided here. Just as I said."

"Can you repeat exactly what you said at breakfast?"

Constance was exhausted and frightened from what she had just experienced on her return to Gerard House. She was in no mood to indulge Roger Gerard's impulsive whims, but if she told him what he wanted to know, she would be rid of him sooner. Then she could tend to Elizabeth. With less zeal than before, Constance recounted the story of meeting Edward by the stairs.

Roger asked when she finished, "What in the world were you doing in the passageway that night?"

"I was afraid," she said honestly.

"I fully understand how you might be a bit frightened to stay here all alone, but you must realize that Edward was also very distraught that you caught him."

"It appears so."

"My poor brother never has recovered from the trauma of being cast out of the Franciscan brotherhood," he confided softly, ostensibly divulging a well-guarded secret.

Constance stared at him in disbelief. "Are you telling me Edward dedicated himself to the Roman Catholic Church?"

Constance Beechum surprised him with her cleverness.

He nodded his head complacently. "A man must find the path to God wherever he may find it," he quickly answered.

"Your brother, actually took vows of poverty, chastity and obedience to our Lord in heaven?"

Roger fought his own demons at that moment, suppressing laughter as he pictured his brother dressed as a monk and being devoted to any entity but himself."

Righteously he attested, "We mustn't be harsh on those who seek solitude and the face of the Lord through the Roman Catholic Church."

Constance, despite her frightening encounter just an hour past, found the story of Edward intriguing. "Has he spoken to you or his wife of the reasons for his expulsion?"

Roger shook his head. "That secret remains his alone, and I'm afraid it has made him the bitter man you see." He sighed glumly. "So now you know more of Edward's story, but please, I urge you not to discuss the matter with my mother. It would so upset her."

129

"Fear not, I will not utter a word of it," Constance said.

"Now you see my urgency in coming to your room to explain this sad situation to you heart-to-heart. I thought long and hard on whether to reveal this state of affairs to you."

Constance could do naught but temper her views of Roger. "It is I who should apologize to both of you for being so harsh."

"Well, shall we now, from this moment on, attempt to trust each other more?" He bent down, grasped her hand and planted upon it a soft kiss. "Now, I must be gone. I suspect mother needs your administrations."

He went to the door and nonchalantly walked out, leaving Constance completely bewildered. Once outside, he leaned against a wall out of her sight and quietly gave way to the laughter he had fitfully stored inside his gut.

As soon as Roger was able to contain his euphoria, he made his way to his brother's room. He knocked on the door with enthusiasm and called out loud.

"The door is open," Edward called back.

Catherine stood at the huge fireplace, taking a sip of sherry. Edward sat in one of the wing chairs, absent-mindedly rubbing his chin with his hand. "Catherine and I have been waiting for you."

"I have something wonderful to share with you," Roger said, closing the door behind him.

"I want no part of your conniving thoughts and scheming. Catherine has learned something explosive." Edward stood up and edged closer to his brother, staring into his curious eyes with such an unsettling intensity that Roger recoiled. "The wench has been visiting George Kane and she's having an illicit affair with the dandy!"

For once in his life, Roger Gerard was stunned into silence. He stared slack-jawed at his brother. Edward raucously laughed in his face.

"I do believe you have lost your wit and your voice. We have the bitch where we want her. It will give me much joy to expel her from the premises immediately."

Roger suddenly realized that his delicious little plan—to use Constance's influence with Elizabeth to sway her into a place in the Will—was unraveling.

"Now let's take a moment to consider other possibilities," he urged. He cast a suspicious look toward Catherine, then back to Edward. "What proof do you have of this affair? You cannot indict a woman for such promiscuous actions without evidence to back up your accusations."

"I observed them sharing an embrace and a kiss." Catherine swallowed the last of the sherry from her glass, placing it on the fireplace mantle. "I watched her leave the house and I then followed her to Kane's cottage—in threatening weather, I should add. I tiptoed to the window and, no doubt, would have seen more if I hadn't tripped and made a racket. I had to rush away and hide on the side of the cottage. I never thought I would be thankful for such foul weather, but the wind prevailed and efficiently covered up my tracks."

Roger felt his ego deflate as if he'd been punctured by Catherine's words. The stupid wench had spurned his advances only to run into the arms of a disgraceful dandy with nothing to offer. This new turn of events could unravel everything he had so cleverly orchestrated. He wasn't going to let a lowly wench like Constance Beechum slap him in the face and run into the arms of George Kane, taking his chance at getting a slice of his mother's Will with her.

"Now let's use common sense here," he said as he paced between Catherine and Edward. A new plan was sprouting as he spoke. "Suppose we can use this information against both Constance and George Kane? We detest the dandy and question his relationship with Mother, and the way he's wormed his way into the family."

Roger grew more excited as he spoke. He so loved a good game. He knew he would have to calm the beast raging in his brother's chest, and his desire to boot Constance out of the house immediately. That would be no simple task. Catherine would be easier to sway to his side. "We should discuss a plan that will be of mutual interest to the three of us."

"There is nothing further to discuss," Edward huffed.

Roger chuckled arrogantly, and his eyes crinkled with unrestrained merriment. "You know that you shall share whatever treasure Mother bequeaths to you, whether or not it is designated in her Will."

"Get out!" Edward raged as he pointed to the door. Catherine merely laughed.

"I will leave when I am done and I will not be done until I have my say." He ran his hand over his stubbled chin. "I have just left Miss Beechum's room. To your mother's nurse, you are now a former Franciscan monk."

"What?"

"I told a great story about you and how you were expelled from a Catholic monastery. She believes it, but I know the truth. I have been to London and I have witnessed a Black Mass." He put a hand in the air and paced the room. "Now, I am not going to question why you should follow such inclinations, but if Mother should find out, well—" He paused and sneered. "I could, of course, be persuaded not to whisper a word of the truth to Mother. That is, if you make the necessary provisions to support me in my customary leisurely lifestyle in London or some other far away place."

The atmosphere in the room became charged. Roger could see Edward trembling with unreleased rage.

"How dare you attempt to blackmail me!" Edward spat.

"Oh, darling, don't be such a bore." Catherine stepped away from the fireplace and became a barrier between the two men. "Personally, I'm rather fond of Roger's intriguing plan. Besides, I'd like to know what he plans to do to that poor excuse for a man, dandy George Kane."

132

Roger smiled smugly. "Ahh, Catherine, my sweet sister-in-law, I know you detest Mr. Kane because the effeminate little bastard brushed off your best flirtations, but that is beside the point. Any reason for revenge is certainly worthy of consideration."

"I will not be part of this circus," Edward said. "I will have that woman out of this house tonight."

"And I will join Roger in your mother's room to validate his tale of your satanic practices." Catherine's voice was serious and filled with venom.

Edward glared a few seconds at both his wife and brother, then he turned away to face the fire. "I have no choice, it seems."

"I don't have to remind you," Roger said, "that with Catherine as my witness, I will succeed. Should you change your mind and think me too big an expense to spare—and if you contemplate, shall we say, removing me as your obstacle—I will make sure to leave enough evidence behind to have you hung for your dark, demented little rituals."

Edward turned and stared with the blazing contempt in his eyes aimed directly at his brother. "What about the wench?"

Roger raised an eyebrow in question.

"Yes, she has apparently accepted your stupid little story for now, but who knows when she'll begin to question its authenticity?"

"Do not fret so much, Roger said. "I will make sure George Kane never crosses Miss Beechum's thoughts again. I will have that delicious wench for my own, and we shall all live happily ever after...once Mother is gone."

Catherine remained silent, but Edward walked to face his brother, nose-to-nose. "I loathe relinquishing myself to you. It goes against my better judgment."

"I must say, it feels rather empowering," Roger said with a sneer. His eyes locked with his brother's in a fierce scowl.

"I have underestimated you," Edward finally admitted.

With a pleased smile, Roger departed the room.

By the time Constance finally entered Elizabeth's room, it was well past supper time. She'd lost track of the days Marguerite, the maid, worked, so she said a silent prayer that she had taken care of feeding the dying woman.

She was relieved to find Marguerite—who always seemed to have stray hairs poking out from her crooked mop cap—removing the food tray from the table.

"Oh, Miss Constance, thank goodness you've returned. Mistress has been restless and asking for you." She rolled her eyes toward Elizabeth.

"I am sorry to be away from here for so long, Marguerite. Thank you for preparing her food. Did she eat much of her supper?" Constance noticed that most of the food on the platter was untouched.

"No, Miss. She said she wasn't hungry."

"That is fine. Thank you, Marguerite. Why don't you leave the tray and I will see if I can entice Elizabeth to nibble a bit."

"I am neither deaf nor dead yet," Elizabeth said from her bed. "I can hear you both. Now go on, Marguerite. Constance and I have much to discuss." She waved the maid away.

As soon as Marguerite was gone, Elizabeth motioned for Constance.

"Come here, child. I've practically exhausted myself waiting for you to get back. What kept you so long?"

If only Constance could tell her everything, but she'd decided not to mention anything of the shots fired at her for fear it might agitate another seizure. She'd even debated revealing what wondrous things had transpired between Georgina and her. The thought of her granddaughter having such a scandalous affair with her nurse might cause the woman to throw her out of the house even quicker than Edward. Worse yet, maybe she'd have her arrested.

"I am afraid the weather took a turn for the worse, and I was delayed in getting back with the expediency I intended. I do apologize." It was partially a truth.

With ancient, well-trained eyes that seemed to see right through Constance, Elizabeth studied her facial expression with keen interest. "Forget that, what happened with my Georgina? I want to know everything."

"I'll take your temperature, and then we'll make sure you eat some of this enticing food."

"I won't eat a bite until you tell me what you and Georgina discussed. I'll have you know, I am feeling better now than I have in days."

Constance knew there was no delaying the details. Elizabeth was more determined than she'd ever seen her. She smoothed out the darling woman's blanket, and smiled when she daydreamed of the warm, tender lips of Georgina Gerard.

"We did not discuss much, Elizabeth, but we promised to meet again soon." Constance wanted to steer the conversation along another path.

"Why does Georgina not visit you here more often? Will she be joining us tonight?"

Elizabeth sighed. "Not today. She has much work to do on the lighthouse restoration."

Constance could not control her short burst of laughter.

"Pray, what is so humorous about that?"

"I just wonder about what Georgina refers to as work," Constance answered. "If I didn't know from you that her work was the restoration of the lighthouse, I would guess that she has a different calling altogether."

"Indeed. And what would you imagine my granddaughter doing?"

Constance walked to the window and remembered the maps, sextant, and protractor scattered on Georgina's desk.

135

She turned back to face Elizabeth. "I fear you will think me quite silly."

"And perhaps I won't."

She stared out the window again. The skies had cleared. "Maybe it comes from a hidden desire to romanticize her, but I would suppose Georgina might be a mysterious sea captain." Again, she faced Elizabeth. "So, now you see how foolish a woman's idle thoughts can be."

Elizabeth began to laugh, but coughing overtook her and shook her tiny body. Constance reached for the glass of water Marguerite had left on the bedside table. The older woman waved her off.

"Perhaps you should not make me laugh so often, my amusing companion. I shall have to mention your wild imaginings to my granddaughter when I next see her. I believe she will find you to be as humorous as I have. I hope you two will become great friends."

"Oh, please do not tell her!" Constance exclaimed. She dashed from the window to stand beside Elizabeth. She was afraid her waggish ramblings would ruin everything so early in their relationship. "I fear it will only make me look the fool in her eyes."

"And you would prefer to appear otherwise?" Elizabeth searched her face.

Constance nodded slowly.

"Then worry not, my Constance. I will not say a word."

"Now I feel more foolish."

"You are only speaking like a woman who is smitten."

Constance opened her mouth but nothing came out. What could she say? Even more troubling, what had Elizabeth just inferred?

"I may be dying, but do you not think I did not see how Georgina avoided your eyes when she wanted nothing more than to touch you?"

"I have not noticed." Constance lied and felt instantly like the deceiver she was. She felt the devil's color rush to her face and hoped Elizabeth did not notice.

"I know my granddaughter better than I know my two sons. She is not like the rest of us, but who am I to interfere with her life? It was a bad lot she was thrown into, and I have done my best to provide for her as she grew into a beautiful young woman. Her life is hers now." She stopped and looked steadily at Constance. "When she looked at you, her eyes betrayed her thoughts."

"Then I am happy that I did not notice her glances," Constance said, feeling more ill as she continued her lies. When would be a good time to reveal the truth to the dying woman? In her death bed? Perhaps now would be more expedient.

"I will not question your own needs and life experiences," Elizabeth said, "but you had to know everything about Georgina. I became aware of her—" She paused. "—differences while she grew up with the only family I could trust to raise my granddaughter. Wilhelmina and Thomas Kane were kind and loving foster parents, but they had only three boys of their own and Georgina mimicked them in most every way. They have a farm on the east end of Castine. They dressed and treated Georgina like another one of their boys. She was climbing trees and playing with wooden toy soldiers rather than making dolls, cooking, and mending clothes. They even dressed Georgina in the boys' hand-me-downs."

Constance would not interrupt her to say that she had not been raised as a boy, yet she was like Georgina in so many ways. No, it was something only God knew the reasons for and why they were different. Why should she question something she was not intended to understand?

Elizabeth clutched her chest and bit her bottom lip, her eyes scrunched shut to hide discomfort. "Now, can you be a good nurse and clear the supper tray from my bed. I will require my laudanum very soon."

"Yes, of course, Elizabeth." Constance was suddenly overwhelmed with conflicting emotions. Even as she felt euphoria when she thought about Georgina, she sadly watched Elizabeth in the grips of so much pain. It was almost too much to bear.

CHAPTER 16

"And how is my sweet mother today?" Roger asked, as he stepped into her bedroom.

Elizabeth seemed surprised to see him. "I've just taken my laudanum for the morning so I'll be asleep soon."

"Well, it is a beautiful day outside." He shifted his attention to the chair beside Elizabeth's bed where Constance sat. "The wind has died down, the snow has stopped and the sun is out. It is a perfect day for a walk or to take a trip."

Elizabeth looked at Constance and smiled faintly. "Constance, you should go out and take advantage of this beautiful day. I will be sleeping soundly when you get back. Go on, now. I won't take no for an answer."

What Constance wanted was to run into the crushing embrace of Georgina. But she had to admit that the sun shining through the window was welcoming and beckoned to her.

"Yes, I believe I would like that very much," she said. "I'll go fetch my bonnet and coat."

After grabbing her outer garments from her bedroom, Constance rushed to meet Roger downstairs. He already held the door open for her at the bottom of the steps. He wore a deep grey coat, polished black boots, and a coach hat on top of his head. As soon as they were outside, he possessively claimed her arm and guided her down the stone steps. "I am at your command, Miss Beechum. Where would you like to walk?"

"Oh, I don't really care. The day is really quite lovely."

"Indeed, lovely enough that perhaps we should take a sleigh and head to Castine for the day?"

"Oh, that sounds delightful!" Not so long ago, Constance had spent a snowy afternoon stuck in Castine's only inn while she waited for a ride to Gerard House. Now she looked forward to seeing the rest of the town.

Roger had arranged for Grayson to harness a horse to a sleigh that waited on the other side of the house. Had he had this planned all along? He carefully wrapped a blanket around her feet before he took the seat beside her. "There you go! We are off! He laughed and gently flicked the horse with the reins.

To get to Castine, they had to go past Lighthouse Pointe and the cottage.

"Say, suppose we take a brief stop at Mr. Kane's cottage? He has not been seen around lately, and I would like to check on his safety."

"I suppose the weather could have kept him away, but I feel sure he's doing just fine." The last thing Constance wanted to do was show up at Georgina's cottage with Roger Gerard. She had to change his mind. "I am really anxious to get to Castine. Can't we visit Mr. Kane another afternoon?"

"We'll only be a moment, my dear. I promise not to spoil our trip to Castine." He smiled at her, but what she saw was the grin of a shark. The sleigh glided effortlessly on the smooth, packed snow and the white snow glistened like tiny diamonds before them.

Soon, they were at the front of the cottage and Roger pulled back on the reins, bringing the horse and sleigh to a full stop. Snow had collected on the rooftop and all appeared peaceful but for the pounding surf below.

"Mr. Kane!" Roger shouted. "Mr. Kane, you have visitors!"

There was only silence.

Roger called out again. He looked at Constance. "Do you imagine there could be trouble?"

Constance shrugged, feeling increasingly uncomfortable. "Perhaps he has gone off to enjoy the day as well," she suggested. "We should continue on to Castine."

Roger swung himself out of the sleigh. "I believe we should take a minute to look inside. He may be ill and unable to holler out. We would be derelict in our Christian duty to not make sure all is well." He looked up at her, waiting for her to agree with him.

Constance gave in. She might find herself in a very precarious position if she continued to disagree with him. He might become suspicious and cause a multitude of problems for both her and Georgina. She had to play along for now.

"Of course." She forced a smile. "How thoughtless of me not to consider Mr. Kane's welfare."

He put his hands around her waist and gently lifted her from the sleigh. Once she was on the snow next to him, he did not release her. His face was but a few inches from hers and she prepared to slap him if he attempted to kiss her. Instead, he released her and took her hand, pointing to the steps of the cottage.

"Come, Miss Beechum."

He called out for George Kane again as they stood on the porch. Still, there was no answer. He went for the door but Constance put a hand out to stop him.

"Do you not think Mr. Kane would be angered if we entered without his invitation?"

"Nonsense!" Roger insisted. "He is our tenant. Besides, how will we find out if he is ill or just out for the day if we do not enter?"

141

She could hear the impatience in his voice. Maybe if she dashed all his ideas, he would be so frustrated that he'd drop this charade and continue on to Castine. Before she could offer any further objections, Roger opened the door and entered the cottage. He turned back to Constance, who was still standing on the porch.

"Well, come in." He extended his hand.

"I don't think—"

He pulled her gently across the threshold. "Now that we are in," he said, "and Mr. Kane is obviously not here nor in bad health, we might tarry a few minutes and warm ourselves before continuing on our journey."

The fire was low, so there wasn't any warmth to be gained from staying longer. Constance felt like they were intruding on Georgina's privacy and wanted to get out of the cottage fast.

Roger stepped to the door and closed it behind him. Then he strolled slowly through the house, surveying the main room and the single bedroom. His concentration locked on the crossed rapiers that hung above the fireplace mantle.

"I had no idea Mr. Kane is a fencer."

"Nor did I," Constance added. "Shall we go now? It is obvious Mr. Kane does not need our concern and we are merely trespassing at this point."

Roger ignored her and caught sight of the desk that was still covered with the maps, sextant and protractor that Constance and seen during her last visit.

"Odd," he murmured as he strolled to the desk to get a better look at the instruments.

"What is odd?" Constance suddenly felt her insides go cold, and the unexplainable feeling that she had to stop Roger from intruding on those things became overpowering.

"These instruments—" he said, pointing to the desk. "Well, I would not expect to find these instruments in the home of a man whose job is to restore a lighthouse made of stone and mortar. These are instruments used on a ship to navigate waters."

Constance walked quietly to stand beside him and got a better look at the huge map spread atop the desk. Roger picked up the map and studied it intently. "This is a map of the east coast of our colonies. What a queer thing for him to have about the house. And there are small markings over the ocean." He held it up closer to his eyes. "I think I can read the writing. They're names: President, United States, Essex, Wasp."

"What was that?" Constance was attempting to read over his shoulders.

"There are names penned on the map here," Roger told her. "I wonder what they could mean?"

She shrugged. "Probably some sort of scientific jargon."

Roger moved away from the table gradually. Short of grabbing him by the coat lapels, she could think of nothing to drag him away. Was he doing this on purpose? Did he suspect something? She didn't think anyone other than Elizabeth knew what was going on, but still...

"Have you seen any evidence of Mr. Kane's actual restoration on the lighthouse?"

"No."

He became pensive. "I dare say, neither have I. Our enigmatic Mr. Kane appears to be a man of many talents, and it is perplexing to discern just who and what he is by merely looking at him." He smiled. "I adore puzzles!"

Constance was on the verge of panic. Roger's words were convincing her more and more that he might know something. What was she to do?

"Please, Mr. Gerard. I've grown nervous, and I really think we have stayed too long. We should take our leave."

"Yes, I suppose." He joined her at the opposite side of the room. "We shall leave, but first, you must hear me out."

"Must we discuss it here and now? We are standing in someone else's home."

143

"Since I first met you," he whispered, "I have wanted to have you alone, away from prying eyes at Gerard House." He took hold of her hand. "And here we are, alone at last."

It was inevitable that he was going to be slapped if he proceeded.

"We must—"

"Constance," he said, using her proper name to give emphasis to his whispered words. "I have been bursting to tell you how much you mean to me."

Constance had to somehow diffuse the situation before it got out of hand. "I never imagined that you would look at me as anything other than your mother's nurse when I arrived at Gerard House."

He shook his head slowly. "I see you as the woman of my heart. You fulfill my dreams. I sense you are a kindred spirit, and I think you are feeling something for me as well."

If only he knew how off target he was. Constance wanted no part of him or any other man.

How could she get out of this situation without hurting his feelings and causing bad blood between them?

She smiled sweetly, but she turned away from him. "I really enjoy your company and friendship, Roger, but I am your mother's nurse. My patients and my profession will always come first. There is time for little else."

"I admire that," he said in a strained voice. "Will you forgive me for thinking more?"

She turned back to face him. He had a sad look in his eyes.

"There is nothing to forgive."

Without warning, he grabbed her and held her in a close embrace. She felt his breath when he implored, "What must I do to have you love me?"

Startled and fearful, Constance struggled against him. "Please, release me now, Mr. Gerard."

CHAPTER 17

Georgina was down on the beach below her cottage and the lighthouse when she saw the sleigh stop at the cottage. Her first thought was that her grandmother had finally succumbed and she left immediately. That meant the American sloops off shore would be left waiting for her return signal. She had been covertly helping them avoid the British brigades that were wreaking havoc against American sailors and shipping.

At that moment in time, her grandmother was more important.

She quickened her pace up the rocky path until she was just a few feet from the cottage. That's when she noticed the empty sleigh. Whoever had come was now inside her home without an invitation. She felt as if her heart jumped into her throat when she realized she'd left all of her maps, charts and navigational equipment on her desktop.

Georgina moved with extraordinary caution, hoping to learn who was lying in wait before she confronted them face-to-face. She lingered at the closed door, listening, but could hear nothing from inside.

She squared her shoulders, grasped the knob, and shoved the door open just in time to see Constance pulling away from Roger Gerard. Georgina was too astonished to speak. She stood silent, her slouch hat shielding her eyes. The door crashed against the wall and the sound reverberated through the room. Constance's face was flushed with embarrassment, but Roger calmly grinned at her.

"What are doing here?" Georgina's anger mounted. The sight of Constance evading the arms of that pompous uncle set off a deep-seated rage she struggled mightily to squelch.

"We were on the way to Castine to take in the town," Roger said smoothly.-"We decided to pay you a surprise visit."

"Is it your normal practice to invade other people's homes?"

"We called out, but you did not answer," Constance said, her eyes pleading for forgiveness.

"Since I did not answer, was it not obvious that I was not here?" she said curtly. "Please leave the premises directly."

Constance felt as if a big, giant rock had crashed into her stomach and sunk there. She gazed steadily at Georgina who would not look at her.

"May I remind you, Mr. Kane, that this cottage belongs to my family," Roger said.

"I am only too aware of that, Sir, but I have rental papers with your mother, and I will not have it used as a—" She paused and flashed an angry gaze toward Constance. "I will not have my home used as a place for lustful trysts."

Constance's mouth dropped open and she stared blankly at Georgina. Roger's cheeks reddened.

"You do not have the right to prevent any member of my family from entering this property, with or without your approval."

"That is not so," Georgina said sharply. "My lease is a legally binding contract with Mrs. Elizabeth Gerard. That contract expressly forbids any person—including members of the Gerard family—from entering my cottage without prior permission."

"I'm certain that does not include members of my family," Roger said angrily, his eyes glaring.

Georgina stood defiantly before him, hands braced on her hips. "I suggest that you speak with your mother's attorney and review the stipulations of our agreement. Apparently you have not been apprised of the particulars." Georgina was fairly confident that Roger preferred to keep his recent exploits hidden from the lawyer's scrutiny. She prayed this smoke screen would prevent him from further snooping, at least until the details of her grandmother's Will were divulged.

"Please, Mr. Gerard," Constance said softly, "let us be on our way, and leave Mr. Kane to his privacy."

Roger ignored her plea. "I do not care for this man's impertinence," he said, speaking to Georgina, not Constance.

"Call it what you wish," Georgina told him. "I am completely within my legal rights to demand that you leave my house immediately."

"And if I were to refuse?"

"I am not a violent man, Roger, but do not test my limits."

"It appears that you put too much value on your privacy. I have to wonder if there is a reason for so much secrecy and isolation."

Prickles ran the length of Georgina's spine. "My desire for solitude is none of your business." She spoke with purposeful calmness. "By nature, I prefer to lead a quiet life—but since you come seeking undeserved explanation, I will acquiesce if it will make you disappear. The truth is, I have very little use for men or women." She looked straight at Constance. "Now, go away."

"Ha!" Roger exclaimed. "Whenever a man hides from the world, you can be assured that some wench is sure to be the cause."

"Please leave my house immediately," Georgina said forcibly.

Roger replied, "In my good time, good fellow. In my own good time."

"I insist, once again. Go!"

Roger ignored Georgina and walked to her cluttered desk. "Your interests, Mr. Kane, are obviously not confined only to the restoration of Lighthouse Pointe. For example, take this map here—of what use would you have for it? And these navigational tools as well?"

"I have a keen interest in ocean currents."

Roger wheeled around. "Currents, you say? Why?"

Georgina's large, almond-shaped green eyes drilled into her inquisitor, but she did not answer him.

"And what are these names on the map?" Roger asked.

"That will be quite enough, Mr. Gerard!"

"My, my, Mr. Kane. What is it about my question that stirs your anger so easily?"

"You are making a very serious mistake," Georgina said, tightly. "Do not continue to provoke me."

"Oh, am I?" Roger said. He turned to Constance. "I do believe this fop must be taught his proper place."

"Mr. Gerard, let him be and let us leave," she implored. "Mr. Kane has every right to be affronted by our actions in his home." She averted Georgina's scorching look of disdain.

"Well, I think not," he said with a narrow smile. Without warning, he cunningly moved to the fireplace and removed the two swords from the wall. "Here!" He tossed one out to Georgina. "Let us see how willing you are to defend your precious home, Mr. Kane!" He flexed the thin blade before him until the steel sang. Then he slashed the air in front of him arrogantly.

Georgina did not seem affected by Roger's superfluous actions. She stood sturdily with the blade poised in readiness.

"Now, Mr. Kane," Roger taunted, "I will teach you some manners."

Constance jumped forward and protectively put her hand on Georgina's arm. "Please, you must not—"

Georgina smoothly shoved her aside. "I have my honor to defend," she said sharply, her eyes still set on Roger.

Roger assumed the classic fencing stance. "If you are ready, en garde!"

Georgina countered, "You are much less than a man, Roger Gerard!"

Constance gasped as Roger thrust at Georgina, but the lunge was parried expertly.

"Please!" Constance cried out, "This is no way to settle anything!"

For an instant, Georgina's gaze locked on the eyes of Constance, and she could not help but want to take her in her arms. She realized that behaving like two fighting roosters was not the proper way to set things straight—especially since innocent American sailors would continue to be captured and forced to do the bidding of the British monarchy if anything should perchance happened to her. She lowered the rapier.

"Fight, damn it!" shouted Roger. "Fight like a man and do not hide behind those fancy clothes."

"Thank you," Constance mouthed discretely to Georgina, her voice inaudible.

Georgina indignantly tossed her rapier across the room. It clattered loudly as it landed on the floorboards behind Roger.

"Coward!" Roger shrieked. "You are but a little boy, not near a man!" He stepped forward and lightly jabbed Georgina's stomach with the rapier. "I could kill you right now."

"I will not fight you," she said, tempering her rage.

Roger backed off, flourished his blade and said, "I will interpret this refusal as your submission to my right to enter this cottage, or any property on Gerard land, without your permission."

Georgina stood silent.

"Very well, I will now depart. Good day, Mr. Kane." Roger offered his arm for Constance's acceptance. She hesitated.

Instead, she stumbled to one of the chairs and flopped herself in it.

"I feel a faint coming on. I will not be able to continue on with you, Mr. Gerard. I would prefer to stay and rest, if Mr. Kane will allow me to do so."

Roger stood stunned, his mouth agape.

Georgina looked at her earnestly. "As a gentleman, it is my duty and honor to offer you my hospitality while you recover, Miss Beechum."

Constance put a hand on her forehead and cast Roger a weak expression. "I am certain Mr. Kane will walk me back to Gerard House once I recover. I know you won't mind, Mr. Gerard." She gave him the sweetest smile she could muster.

"I will not leave without you, Miss Beechum. We came together and we shall leave together." He shot Georgina a defiant glance.

"Do you think it wise?" Georgina asked. "Do you intend to force an ill woman to ride in a cold sleigh? What if she succumbs to a fever and becomes even more ill? That would only delay her return to your dear, sick mother. Although, I am most certain that Edward or his wife—or certainly your gallant self—would willingly tend to sweet Elizabeth's needs.

She turned her attention back to Constance. "Would you like to reconsider? Perhaps the sleigh ride—"

"Wait!" Roger gazed first at Georgina, then more steadfastly at the fading Constance. "Very well...I hope I do not regret this decision, but I warn you—" He pointed at Georgina. "Look after her and get her back to Gerard House as soon as she is feeling better."

He went to Constance and took her hand gently. "I apologize, my dear, for not keeping my promise to visit Castine. We shall do it again soon." He glared one more time at Georgina, then walked out without uttering another word.

Georgina followed him to the porch and watched until the sleigh was far distant, following along the path back to Gerard House.

"I thought he would never leave." Constance stood by the fireplace, untying her bonnet and removing her coat.

Georgina took off her hat and flung it on the table. Constance smiled hesitantly. "Georgina, allow me to explain."

The other woman took off her coat, her gaze never leaving Constance. She crossed her arms across her chest and leaned against the fireplace mantle.

"So, you were acting? You're not really ill. I'm quite willing, Miss Beechum, to hear you out on why you were here, in my home, where I welcomed you openly. Why did I find you alone and in the arms of my uncle?"

Constance, stunned by the icy tone in Georgina's reply, rushed to her and placed both hands on her shoulders. Georgina did not back away.

"Do not treat me with such cold indifference. I have been able to think of nothing but being back in your arms since I left you yesterday. At the very least, allow me to explain what happened."

Georgina's green eyes searched her face and Constance caught a flicker of tenderness, but then her jaw tightened and she lifted her chin in defiance.

"I have eyes that saw very well what was happening in my home."

Constance, frightened and frustrated at the thought of losing the one true love she thought she'd never find, took Georgina's face in her hands and peered into her eyes.

"Please, my darling, gaze into my eyes and study me closely. I do not favor the male persuasion. I have fallen in love with only two women in my life, one who broke my heart and one who I am praying will not break it again. Hear me out and think about what you did not see when you came into the room. Did you not realize I was pushing the man away? Roger used the excuse to come here because he thought you were ill. Lies he used to not only push himself on me, but also to spy on you."

151

Georgina's eyebrows creased with concern. "He suspects me of what? Do you think he has discovered my disguise?"

"I do not know, but you must believe me when I say that I tried everything within my limited powers to get him to leave when we discovered you were not here. He has been wooing me since I arrived." Constance backed away from Georgina and stood watching the fading fire. "He fully believes that I will fall under his spell and into his bed. When we found ourselves here and alone, he took advantage of the situation and forced his amorous intentions upon me. I was fleeing from his grasp when you rushed through the door."

Constance suddenly felt exhausted. She didn't know if it was the heat from the fireplace, but she thought she could really faint. She feared Georgina would not believe her.

She was grabbed by gentle hands as Georgina turned her around to face her. She wiped away some of the tears that had spilled down Constance's cheeks.

"Constance, will you accept this foolishly impulsive woman's apology?" She pulled Constance into her arms and held her in a tight embrace, eyes locked on her. "Forgive me. I am like a giddy child filled with passion and emotions for you that I am not certain how to handle." She planted a light kiss on Constance. "I give you my heart, Constance Beechum, but there are so many things I wish to know about you."

Constance was certain her cheeks were ready to explode they felt so hot, and her entire body felt as if she were floating away like a stray ember.

"My darling," she said, "I have kept my heart under lock and key after Lily, but I have opened the door and am ready to give myself to you." She knew what those words meant and she was ready.

She reached behind Georgina and found the clasp holding back her shimmering, raven tresses. She pulled the cascading hair down, spreading it like a mantle around Georgina's shoulders and across her face.

She could not take her eyes off the beautiful woman before her and tried to keep the fire coursing through her body under control. "You are the most beautiful, fake man I've ever met." She smiled and winked at Georgina.

Georgina leaned down and smothered her with a deep, passionate kiss. Constance thought she would drown in euphoria and the fire from that kiss. When they parted, Georgina still held her tightly.

"Tell me about Lily," she whispered in Constance's ear.

The last thing Constance wanted to do was talk about Lily Sinclair. She was so hot that she fully believed the fire from the fireplace had set her ablaze. What she desired more than anything at this extraordinary moment was for Georgina Gerard to make passionate, reckless love to her.

"Lily is my past, Georgina, but if you wish, I will tell you about her. She was the daughter of my employer. I worked as a milliner, stuck like a prisoner in the hot, back room of a busy hat shop, turning out hats like a production line. Lily and I became very close friends because most of the other workers were older women. She would arrange for us to spend time alone at break times and even after hours for tea. She was forever flirty, fluttering her eyes at me and touching my arms sensuously. I believed her when she told me she liked me more than just a friend, and that I meant the world to her..."

Constance paused, not realizing how raw the memories still were. She wanted to pull away from Georgina because the heat and passion were too strong, but Georgina would not let her go.

"Do not continue if the memories are still too painful," Georgina said gently.

Constance shook her head and smiled at her. "No, they are not really painful, just unbelievable." She offered a big smile to Georgina. "I really don't wish to speak of Lily Sinclair. Let me just finish by saying that I found out she was engaged to be married to the son of a wealthy banker. That is when she tossed me off, like an old hat. She threatened to reveal my advances toward her to her mother, if I did not leave their employ. All at once, I became loveless, jobless and penniless. I believe she did indeed spread evil rumors because I was a damn good hat maker, but suddenly no one would open their doors to me."

She placed her head upon Georgina's chest, feeling drained from the recounting of her affair with Lily and feeding off the other woman's steady heartbeat. "Don't let me go, please," she whispered.

Without saying a word, Georgina whisked Constance off her feet and held her firmly in her arms as she made her way to her bedroom.

"Shall I tie you to my bed, then?" They both laughed and then kissed again, tasting eagerly of each other's mouths.

CHAPTER 18

"And what makes you brood so?" Edward asked as he walked into the large sitting room to find Roger nursing a full glass of wine. "You've barely put your lips to the wine." His voice was mocking.

Roger only glared at him.

"I thought that you would be preening your colorful feathers like a proud peacock after your easy conquest of Miss Beechum." He took a sip of the sherry that he'd just poured. He looked deviously over the edge of his glass. "The poor girl must be exhausted. So too must you be, the way you're acting now. I tell you, she does not even answer her door. Catherine is now sitting with Mother in her stead."

"There was no conquest," Roger said tersely.

"No conquest?" Edward nearly spit out his sherry. "So that is the reason for your gloom, then? How could you be refused?"

"I advise you to just shut up, Edward!" Roger leapt from the chair. "It is hard to hear my thoughts with you prattling."

Edward narrowed his brows. "Be careful of your place."

Roger dropped back into the chair.

"And where is the wench now? Elizabeth has been asking after her."

Roger eyed his brother. "We stopped at the cottage at Lighthouse Pointe and she had a fainting spell. I left her with Mr. Kane until she recovered."

Edward burst into boisterous laughter. "Bravo, my little brother! Not only did you deliver her directly to your rival for her hand, but you craftily left her in the arms of her lover. That is certainly an efficient way of getting Mr. George Kane out of the way, eh? If only I were so cunning."

Roger only glared. Edward pointed a finger at him. "I warned you not to try to use the woman as a pawn!"

"And what makes you so full of frivolous chatter this evening?" Roger wanted to change the subject.

Edward walked to the large fireplace mantle and drummed his fingers atop it. "You could say there is a deep pleasure in winning even a small victory," he said with a sardonic grin."

Roger furrowed his brows, but not because of his brother's words. No, it wasn't even the fact that he had erased any gain he had made with Constance Beechum. His thoughts were concentrated on George Kane. There was something odd about the man, and what he'd discovered in his cottage gave him much concern.

"My words are falling on deaf ears," Edward grumbled.

Roger said, "I care not one jot about your words."

"Oh? Then you still harbor hope that Miss Beechum will sway mother's mind to your favor?"

Roger reached for the glass of wine at chair's side. Edward smiled broadly. "Now, that is more like my brother."

Roger swiftly drank all that had been poured in his glass. He refilled it again from the decanter, but did not drink. He sat back on the red velvet wing chair and swirled the sherry in its glass as he contemplated what had transpired at the cottage. Any real gentleman would have taken up his challenge. He was certain Mr. Kane was no coward. He also had to admit that it was Constance's words that stayed the man's actions.

Edward chuckled. "One has to wonder...will your wench come home tonight at all, or dare she stay till the morning with the not-so-honorable Mr. Kane?"

Roger ignored him and lifted his glass of wine in a salute to his brother. "If you will stop your prattling about my failure with Constance—" He expertly emptied the sweet wine in one great swallow.

"So, it is Constance now, is it?" Edward raised an eyebrow. "I thought the privilege of using a woman's first name came after carnal relations."

Roger stared at him blankly and seethed.

Edward snickered as he pushed his brother further. "Apparently, she still dangles the fruit of her womanhood before your foolish eyes."

"Will you please refrain from this!" Roger said hotly. "There is something far more important and potentially dangerous to speak about."

"Very well." Edward nodded for him to proceed.

"When we were at Mr. Kane's cottage earlier today—" Roger hurriedly related the afternoon's events to Edward, including all that had taken place and detailing what he had observed on Kane's desk.

"Tell me again—what were the names on the maps and charts?" Edward asked.

Roger repeated each name methodically, according to where they appeared. Then he asked, "Do you have any idea what they stand for?"

"And what reaction did the wench have to all this?"

"Why make such a silly inquiry?"

"Well, if he is her paramour, then she might be involved in whatever he is doing in that cottage." Edward stared at his brother as if he were a child.

Roger shook his head. "She knows nothing. Do not bring her into this."

157

"The names could be anything," Edward said. He pondered what he'd just been told. "Or they could be the names of ships. I am trying to recall titles of the sloops in our Navy."

Roger smacked his forehead with his palm. "By God, I did not think of that possibility! You could be right." He regarded his brother with renewed interest.

Edward was smug. "I can find out the information from my associate in Washington. But what is more important is what that weasel, Kane, could be doing with those maps, and what he intends for the ships indicated on them."

Roger's face lit up. "What if he is a spy?"

Edward eyed him for a moment then shook his head. "No, we know all the British agents. We pay them to keep watch on what our side is doing along the coast. If they were to make it difficult for our British friends to do business here, we'd be penniless. Our lumber sales are the only thing keeping this house and family afloat."

Edward went back for another sherry refill then turned back to Roger. "You are quite right about how important this information is. We cannot afford our operations to be interrupted. Smuggling lumber to the British could very well land us in the brig or worse. We could be labeled as traitors."

"But what do you suppose we do?" Roger asked uneasily.

"For the present, nothing," Edward responded. "Do not relay any part of this conversation to Catherine or mother. We shall wait and keep a very close watch on our tenant, and also the nurse. She may lead us to the solution."

Edward absent-mindedly finished the last drops of sherry and threw his empty glass in the burning fireplace.

"My grandmother will be missing you if I don't get you back to Gerard House before nightfall." Georgina watched

Constance fuss over the fit of her dress. The empire waist and plunging neckline spilled her ample breasts accentuated the top. She herself stood, barely dressed, in pantaloons, and an unbuttoned big sleeved white shirt with a green brocade vest.

"Not as much as I shall miss you, my darling, Georgina." Constance joined her for a final embrace. She could not remove her eyes from the exquisitely shaped, pale bosom of beautiful Georgina. She slipped her hands into her lover's shirt and ran them over each supple breast. How could she ever judge this woman to be a man? She was inclined to forget everything and return to their bed of lovemaking.

"I never thought it would be this perfect," she whispered in a raspy voice. "I shall never have enough of you."

Georgina took her hands and kissed them gently. "My feelings as well, my Constance, but if you persist, I will have the entire Gerard household here with pitchforks to snag you back."

Constance grudgingly released her and let her finish dressing.

"Must you wear that musty old corset to flatten your chest?" she asked. She pointed to the modified foundation garment that had been anxiously draped over a wing back chair.

"Yes," Georgina declared. "It is imperative that no semblance of feminine mounds appear at my chest, darling. I am considered a man, after all." Georgina smiled and shook her head. "I've done very well with the alterations Mrs. Kane made to it. She is a superb foster mother and a seamstress as well."

She grabbed her undergarment and skillfully wrapped it around her figure, tightly lacing the custom-made bodice over her breasts so hard that she winced in pain. "Thank the Lord my mother added the clasps to the front so I would not require assistance in putting this wretched thing on."

"How horrid for you!" Constance said. "Women no longer have use for those things. Don't you like the new empire styles? Do you not even miss wearing feminine clothing?"

Georgina was nearly fully dressed with waistcoat and tailcoat, and was pulling on her boots.

"No. I think I shall dress this way always." She winked at Constance. "Without the corset, of course." She stood up, went to Constance and kissed her deeply and slowly.

"Would you mind if I never wore a dress?" she asked with a mischievous twinkle in her eyes.

"As long as that corset gets burned, I find you unbelievably divine in your dandy attire."

Both Georgina and Constance laughed out loud as they both walked out, holding hands, to the main living room of the cottage. The fire burned low but was not out completely. It was still nice and warm.

Constance was suddenly overwhelmed by sadness and uncertainty. Their lovemaking had been like heaven, and the little bedroom provided an escape into complete bliss from the ugliness of the real world. As she looked around the room, with the two swords still tossed on the floor and the cluster of crumpled maps, charts and instruments on Georgina's desk, she could not put those memories out of her thoughts.

"Georgina," she said as she tied the bonnet under her chin, "what exactly is it that you do with all those maps and naval instruments? Roger seems to suspect you are guilty of something nefarious—or at the least, mysterious."

Georgina had grabbed her coat but stopped and looked at her seriously.

"I suppose grandmother will forgive me if I delay you just a bit longer." She pointed Constance to one of the chairs. "Sit down for a moment."

She sat across from her on the other chair. "I shall be forthright, for I do not wish to hide anything from you. I have lied to you. I am not restoring Lighthouse Pointe. To be honest, I know absolutely nothing about such restorations or

160

even lighthouses." She paused, leaned closer and took hold of Constance's delicate hands. "What I tell you must remain with you until death. Can I trust you, my Constance?" She gazed intently at her.

"Of course, you can trust me." She traced her fingertips over Georgina's face. "What you tell me now remains sealed behind my lips. I would cut my wrists rather than betray your trust." Constance could hear the heavy thudding of her heart in her ears.

"Uncle Roger has every reason to suspect me," Georgina said. "If, like the Gerards, you are in bed with the British Empire—if you are a British sympathizer or a Whig—then I am now confessing to you that I am indeed a spy."

Constance inhaled sharply, but remained still and intently listened to what her lover had to reveal.

"Thank you for not running out the door on me after telling you what I just did." Georgina offered a tepid smile. "When we met for the first time in the coach, I suspected you had a keen interest in our talk of politics and our impending war with the Empire. I don't think I'm wrong?" She left it as a question.

"If it involves you, especially, I am interested," Constance said.

"Well, then...the maps and charts I keep here along with the instrumentation help me keep track of American sloops and also British war ships patrolling our waters off the Maine coast. The redcoats are firing and blocking our ships. They attack and steal away our very own sailors, taking them as prisoners to serve on their own ships, and forcing them into the service of the King of England. Many of our captured men are dying of diseases and poor living conditions."

Constance was at first struck dumb by her lover's revelations, but she could not hold back her questions.

"I have heard some of the men talk of such atrocities and the growing bad blood between our President and the King of England."

161

Georgina nodded. "Well, my darling, I could not sit still and allow this to happen, especially when some individuals are putting our own sailors in danger just to satisfy their own greed—"

"Are you speaking of the Gerard family?"

"My father has been profiting handsomely from the sale of his lumber to the British for the building and repairing of their warships...the very ships that are sinking our own sloops. The Gerard family business prospers while our men are tortured aboard those same ships."

Constance covered her mouth with her hand, her eyes wide open in horrific surprise. "And I thought Edward could not be worse than I imagined."

"I use those maps and charts to keep track of where the British ships are on our coastline, and I then relay their positions to waiting American sloops that are hiding in the cove." She paused and her eyes bore into Constance. "You know about the lights—you have already seen them."

"You are using the lights to communicate the coordinates to our ships!" Constance approvingly shouted with enthusiasm.

"Not only are you beautiful, but you are an intelligent woman as well." Georgina leaned over and kissed her proudly. "Yes, we send code to each other with our lamps. Inside the old lighthouse, I have constructed crude steps fashioned from scraps of lumber and stones that I gathered along the shore. They are just tall enough to get me up to the highest standing point. At nightfall, I use my lamp to relay the coordinates of any British ships that might be on patrol. That way, our sailors can avoid them and also prevent them from conducting business, raiding our ships, and plundering houses along our shores."

Constance jumped up from her chair and threw herself at Georgina, hugging her neck closely. "You are a hero!" She excitedly covered her face with kisses.

Georgina laughed heartily. "Well, I don't know about a hero. Some citizens believe I am aiding our country in bringing a new war with the British Empire to our shores."

Constance was crestfallen as she collapsed back into her chair. "The British fleet patrolling off our shores isn't the only pressing issue that might be dragging us into another war with England. Our President seems intent on plowing ahead and marching into northern territory."

"Aye," Georgina woefully agreed. "He is pushing against the Shawnee tribes and the Indian nation. There most certainly will be a war if Madison continues to satiate his appetite for Canada."

It sounded to Constance as if her Georgina was working for the United States government.

"Are you officially working for President Madison? Are you part of our Navy?" She suddenly grew afraid for Georgina's safety.

"My darling, suppose I promise to tell you everything when we are again lying together in bed? We must get back to Gerard House immediately." Again, she reached over and kissed Constance. "Do you believe that I will always be honest with you?"

How could Constance doubt those piercing, pure and independent eyes? She trusted Georgina Gerard with her life.

"Let us be on our way, my love." Constance kissed Georgina one final time. "My kiss should convey to you my answer, leaving your heart with little to doubt about what I believe and how I feel about you."

CHAPTER 19

Georgina and Constance stood at the rear door to Gerard House. "Why did we come around to the kitchen service entrance?" Constance asked, feeling a bit perplexed. "I do not know if Marguerite is here today to let us inside."

Georgina pulled a key out of her waistcoat pocket and waved it in front of her. "We won't need Marguerite. How do you think I go in and out so freely in Gerard House without a soul seeing me?"

Constance touched her shoulder. "Will you come inside and visit your grandmother?"

Georgina gazed steadily at her and shook her head. "I must not. There are important tasks that I must attend to, and many ideas I should consider before the dinner."

"What are you planning?"

"Grandmother is dying. Doctors and laudanum will not save her life." She did not appear concerned. In fact, her demeanor was that of a high-spirited conspirator. She grinned slyly at Constance. "The masquerade has gone on for long enough. I want nothing more than to put my lips to your mouth right now, but there are spying eyes in this house. We should not risk being exposed."

164

She took Constance's hand and pressed her warm lips to her chilled skin. "I shall see you after the morrow, my love. It will be spectacular." The twinkle in her eyes both amused and worried Constance.

It was heart-wrenching to leave Georgina standing outside, but Constance knew she was right. They couldn't risk losing everything—especially not now, when the stakes were so high and Georgina suspected the culmination of her work was fast approaching.

She found Marguerite running from the blazing hearth to the table where there was chopped vegetables, plucked chickens, and a plump mound of dough sitting about. Her bonnet sat askew upon her head and, as always, stray brown hairs poked out from the edges, at her face and neck.

"Oh, Miss, you gave me quite the scare, you did!" She clapped her hands together to remove flour from her palms, which created wispy white clouds that wafted in the air. She didn't stop working as she spoke with Constance. "When did you start using the kitchen entrance? You're beginning to act like that good looking Mr. Kane." She laughed as she fashioned the risen dough into a loaf on a bread board. When she was satisfied with its shape, she slid it inside a brick oven across the room. "He enjoys his game, he does. He likes to surprise Mistress Elizabeth like that, and he especially enjoys befuddling those Gerard brothers."

This time, she stopped and stared at Constance, who hadn't moved or said a word. She could not get the images of Georgina, resting in her arms, out of her thoughts.

"Well, Miss Constance, you look as if you're clear across the ocean right now." She stood motionless, her thin but strong hands firmly planted on her narrow hips.

Constance shook her head to clear her thoughts and smiled. "I am profusely sorry, Marguerite. My contemplations were indeed in a very beautiful place far away from here." She looked again at the very busy table which was topped with a wealth of food. "Will you be able to handle all of this for the dinner, Marguerite? Would you like me to help you with anything?"

Marguerite's eyebrows arched. "Oh no, I simply could not allow that. If the Gerards knew you were down here, they'd have me thrown out for sure."

Constance frowned. "Nonsense. They wouldn't survive two days without you. Let me at least prepare Elizabeth's food."

Marguerite grudgingly accepted her offer. "Fine, Miss. The Gerards requested that I stay on for the night and I'll stay to prepare the dinner. I'll be here at rooster's call. We can fix Mistress Elizabeth's food early and it'll keep for dinner."

The next day, Constance spent most of her time with Elizabeth. She'd noticed a turn for the worse in the dying woman and feared whether she would be strong enough to withstand the trek downstairs and dinner with the entire family tomorrow and whatever Georgina had planned for the night. Constance avoided taking dinner with Roger, Edward and Catherine without giving them excuses.

Her relationship with Elizabeth had grown even closer after she explained what had transpired between Roger and her granddaughter. "How dare he break into a Georgina's home," she disapproved vehemently when she learned about her youngest son's unconscionable behavior.

As for Constance, she dodged Roger as much as possible. When they did happen to cross paths, he barely spoke and looked at her with melancholy spaniel-like eyes, hoping for sympathy.

The nightmares came back, except this time, she was coming face to face with her own tombstone! Constance dreaded sleep for fear she would dream again of howling blizzards and cloaked demons swirling above her own grave.

Despite the euphoria and all-consuming love she felt for Georgina, she realized that another, quite darker emotion threatened her joy. An ominous brooding enveloped her heart and she feared herself powerless to chase it away.

It was nearly twilight as she stood at the window; the sky had turned grey as lead and the wind buffeted the bare, menacing tree branches. She felt despondent and missed the sultry embraces from Georgina's comforting arms.

Elizabeth called, "Constance?"

She did not hear her.

Elizabeth bade her again.

She returned from her stupor and looked at her sweet patient. "Yes," Constance answered, but her tone betrayed her mood.

"Are you well, child?"

Constance left the window and walked to the bed. "I am sorry."

Elizabeth eyed her. "Has my son Roger anything to do with it?"

"No," she replied, looking at her. "We've barely seen each other, and when we do bump into each other, we have nothing to say."

Elizabeth appeared tired, her eyes growing even more hollow and the color of her skin turning an unhealthy tint. Constance continued to hope that her ministering could make Elizabeth's last days more bearable at the end.

Still, the sick woman looked at her affectionately and managed a weak smile. "Let us speak of more joyous things for a bit of cheer." Her voice was barely a whisper and her hands began to shake. "Tomorrow is our special dinner. I am still hoping you and Georgina will help me down to the dining hall. It is this dying woman's last wish to have supper with her family."

Constance tried to hold back the tears that she could feel coming. She smoothed out Elizabeth's blanket and tucked some loose hairs that had fallen on her face behind her ears.

167

"Of course we shall bring you downstairs. Nothing or no one will keep us from our celebration. Marguerite is preparing quite a feast and I, personally, will prepare your favorite dish. The table will be ablaze with candlelight."

When Constance made sure Elizabeth was fast asleep, she nearly ran all the way across the balcony and to her room on the other side of the house. Her heart was beating fast. The last thing she wanted was to run into any of the Gerards.

She got to her room, bolted the door and stood in her room taking deep breaths. She finally flung herself on the bed to collect her emotions. The excitement over seeing Georgina again was like a drug through her system. But the ever present fear of the unknown kept her heart beating just as hard.

She felt better after a while and stood up, having decided to try on the one and only evening dress she had indulged in with the funds Uncle Merriweather had sent for wardrobe and undergarments. It was her very best dress and it was the one she would wear tomorrow evening.

She quickly removed her simple day dress and removed the pale orchid dress from the hanger. The exquisite silk fabric heightened her naturally ivory complexion and revealed her womanly figure. The dress was cut in the most daring of the French empire fashion, accentuating her full, high breasts and hinting at her well-proportioned hips. Constance feared the deep cut of the dress showed a bit more of her breasts than would be proper, so she had bought a special, snow-white lace scarf to hide the neckline so daringly exposed.

She had no expensive jewelry to set off the ensemble, but Constance had always made do with the one item of jewelry she could never bring herself to sell when she was desperate for money. Her mother's ruby and diamond cross. The chain was delicate and the cross an antique that had been passed down through her mother's family. It would do quite nicely.

She held up the dress in front of her and posed in front of the small, mahogany oval mirror over the wash stand. Even though the fire was dying out in the fireplace, Constance glowed with anticipation. She smiled and wondered how Georgina was going to keep her eyes off of her.

Constance went to bed so drowsy with excitement that no nightmares dared intrude into her dreams.

CHAPTER 20

Constance spent most of the following morning sneaking between Elizabeth's room and Marguerite's kitchen. She made sure to chop up and mash the chicken as fine as possible and added extra seasonings and savory broth. Tonight was special and Constance could not keep the fear of her fading health and the implications of her imminent death from her mind. Elizabeth Gerard would have tasty food and even a drop of wine if she wished tonight.

Catherine had locked herself in her room for the better part of the day, her hair in clips and combs, preparing for the dinner. Constance caught Roger and Edward huddled in the sitting room, deep in conversation. She avoided them and was thankful for whatever held their interest.

Outside, the day was clear and stayed that way until twilight. Poor Marguerite would need an extra day to recover from the grand dinner tonight, and Constance would have to manage the extra day off with Elizabeth on her own.

As the sun disappeared behind the cliffs, Constance was surprised to run into Gray downstairs, standing atop a stool, lighting one of the chandeliers in the large foyer.

"Good evening, Gray. I wasn't expecting to see you." She was pleased to see the older man again.

He glanced down and offered a subdued smile. "Evening, Miss Beechum. Marguerite left word with my Missus that the Mistress was wanting my help in preparing for the dinner tonight. I won't be stayin', just putting some fire to the candles, making sure there's plenty of wood for the fireplaces, and then I'll be on my way." He went back to lighting the rows of candles. Constance was happy to see him, but couldn't suppress a shiver as she remembered the harrowing trip to Gerard House and the hooded figures they had come across on the snowy road. She pushed those unsettling thoughts as far away as possible, and focused on the upcoming evening.

Already, Gerard House was coming alive with the flicker of candlelight. The glow from the light made Constance feel lighthearted and joy washed through her body. When she thought of Georgina, the warmth just intensified.

She was upstairs with Elizabeth, making sure she had tucked every piece of her snowy white hair into a perfect roll on the back of her head, and she smoothed every crease on the older woman's blue velvet dress. The white lace on the collar and long sleeves brought out the richness of its rich royal blue color. Constance stood back and smiled appreciatively at her friend.

"You look absolutely lovely, Elizabeth. You shall be the star of the evening."

Elizabeth waved her off. "Don't be foolish, child, it will be my darling Georgina and you who will shine like stars." Constance held a hand mirror to her face. "See how pretty you are?" The older woman giggled and said, "I am shining already. I feel like I have been given new energy for this old, dying skin, if only for one more glorious night."

A knock on the door interrupted their conversation.

"Who is it?" Constance called out.

"Mr. Kane."

Constance was flabbergasted. She had not yet dressed for dinner and was still in her drab day dress.

Elizabeth's eyes twinkled and she came to life. It was obvious that her granddaughter's arrival revived her spirit. She eagerly motioned Constance to the door. "Well, tell her to come in!"

Constance walked to the door and thought her legs would surely give out at any moment. "Please, come in," she managed to say when she opened the door.

But when she saw Georgina walk into the room, her eyes opened wide in shock and surprise. Georgina was wearing her long hair loose. Its shiny, black curls draped over her ears and settled about her shoulders like a raven mantle. She still wore her masculine attire, and Constance wondered if she was still wearing that dreadful modified corset. She didn't want to stare—it was not proper—but she worried that Georgina might be needlessly uncomfortable.

Georgina smiled coyly. Her emerald green eyes passionately searched Constance's face.

"I pray I have not shocked you into complete silence." She went past Constance to stand beside her grandmother. "You are magnificent tonight." She leaned down and embraced the frail woman gently.

"I don't recollect when I last had an evening like this," Elizabeth announced. Constance had never seen her so animated since she had arrived. It had been a good decision to insist on having Elizabeth come downstairs for a family dinner after Edward and Roger initially denied the dear lady's wishes.

Georgina sat on the bed directly beside her grandmother. Elizabeth reached out and caressed her granddaughter's beautiful hair.

"I will not ask you why you have chosen to come to dinner thus, but I can only guess you have a good reason. You look more like your mother, Beth, tonight, than that man named George Kane. Did you come through the kitchen door?"

Georgina nodded, looking first at Constance and then back at her grandmother. "I did come through the kitchen. Only Marguerite saw me and she had no time, poor thing, to say a word. And I do indeed have an excellent reason why I have not tied back my hair, grandmother. After much consideration, today I have made decisions that I pray will be the right ones. I am playing tonight. I merely want my Father, Uncle and Auntie Catherine to play with me." She winked slyly at Constance, signaling that she should expect a prodigious evening.

The old woman chuckled. "Oh, you know your grandmother loved games when she was a young woman."

Constance could not take her eyes from Georgina. What she wanted desperately was to run her hands through her lover's hair and to smother her with kisses, but instead, she stood away, near the door.

Elizabeth struggled to get up in bed. Georgina helped her by offering a supportive hand at her back.

"Georgina...Constance, why not help me downstairs now? I can hardly control myself locked up in this prison of a room. And Constance, my dear...Once I'm sitting comfortably in the dining hall, why don't you go up to your room and freshen up for the evening?"

Everyone was already seated when Constance arrived downstairs. The moment she entered the dining hall, all eyes were on her. She smiled sweetly, trying desperately not to focus on Georgina's shocked stare, and she bid them each a good evening.

Georgina was instantly on her feet. She moved swiftly to her side, presented her arm and escorted her to the table. Constance could literally feel Georgina's gaze devouring her. She could not bring herself to look at Roger. Edward, on the other hand, barely paid her any attention. His eyes were focused solely upon Georgina.

Poor Marguerite worked so hard as she served each course without a sliver of a smile. Her unruly hair had its way, sticking out of her freshly-starched cap. Constance had to hold herself back from getting up to assist her with the dinner service.

Through most of the dinner, she took little part in the conversation, but nonetheless, enjoyed being there and watching the energy and joy on the face of Elizabeth Gerard. One dinner wasn't going to change the fact that she had little time left, but at least this time with her family had given her a reprieve from the prison of her bed and room.

By the time the platters of meat arrived on the table, she realized that Edward and Roger were silent. Catherine continued to draw the attention of Georgina. Constance still held firm in her belief that the woman held a secret attraction to the man she thought was George Kane. Georgina asked Constance several questions regarding her Uncle Merriweather and his law practice, and Constance did her best to answer.

As dinner wore on, Roger drank more than his share, until Elizabeth stopped him. "Roger, I think you should refrain from any more wine before the end of dinner."

Roger's face was already flushed from all the wine he had downed. It became nearly crimson from his mother's admonition. "I can hold my liquor, Mother," he answered.

Constance fully expected Elizabeth to utter even sharper words, but to her surprise, she said nothing more to her son. Instead, she and Georgina began to talk of Georgina's travels to the Canadian border.

"You have actually been there?" Constance was surprised that Georgina had not mentioned such exciting journeys to her.

"I have been there on several occasions."

"Do the names President, United States, Essex and Wasp have any special significance?" Edward asked out of the blue, to the surprise of everyone at the table.

Constance immediately cast a scowl at Roger. From the smirk on his face, she knew that he had told Edward everything. She looked at Georgina and saw that the question had taken her by surprise as well.

"The names mean nothing to me."

"On the contrary, my brother inadvertently visited your cottage while out with Miss Beechum and came across maps and charts with the odd names written upon them. I gather he has apologized for barging into your house while you were absent...am I correct?"

Georgina swirled the wine in the goblet in front of her. She smiled, switching her attentions between Edward and Roger. "I did not feel the need to explain anything to your brother, but since you asked, I am afraid I must reveal my little secret indulgence." She glanced briefly at both Elizabeth and Constance. "I've taken a liking to writing adventure tales. I've been taking notes to write an epic novel of high sea adventures. I do hope that you will read my book once it is complete." She poured wine from the decanter, offered it to Edward, then drank the sweet nectar from her brimming glass.

Edward lapsed into silence again, taking time to study Georgina closely.

By the time the sumptuous meal had ended, much of the tension was gone. Constance enjoyed listening to Georgina's descriptions of her travels to the Canadian border. She'd even witnessed a Shawnee from afar.

She also relished the fact that Georgina was staring at her even though she was talking to her grandmother. Her gaze studied her face, neck and once settled on her breasts. Constance felt the heat rise to her cheeks and through her body.

Elizabeth seemed to be holding her strength, not appearing to tire as the night progressed. Eventually, she turned her attention back to Edward.

"Edward, I notice you have been scrutinizing Mr. Kane carefully, as have I." She cast her gaze to Georgina. "It is remarkable—with his hair unbound, he bears an uncanny resemblance to someone we once knew. Look closely, Edward. If Mr. Kane were female, he could be kin to Bethany Smythe." She looked steadily at her son. "Don't you think?"

Edward's hand trembled and he almost dropped his wine goblet.

Roger harrumphed and sipped more of his own. "Well, looking at his attire tonight, he might prefer to be of the feminine sex." He looked at his brother. "Who the devil is Bethany Smythe?"

Edward was struck dumb. He only glared at his mother from across the table. Catherine plastered a fake smile on her face and looked Georgina over.

"Well, I can see the coloring, the raven hair and the same green eyes." She looked at Roger. "Bethany Smythe was a scullery maid that worked here many years back. I have no idea why my mother-in-law would bring that woman up."

"I am intrigued," Georgina said slowly. "Did Bethany Smythe have any children?"

Suddenly, the intrigue came together for Constance. She knew what Georgina was up to. Wearing her hair down was something purposeful she had done to bring this very conversation to the table. And Elizabeth was now most definitely in on the game.

"Unfortunately not," Elizabeth said. "She met an untimely death when she fell over the cliff just on the other side of Lighthouse Pointe, near twenty-three years ago."

Roger set his wine glass down hard on the table. He was without a doubt, filled with entirely too much wine. "Well, this is a totally mundane conversation. I've had my fill of this

176

dinner." He wore a crooked smile and looked like he could tip over on the table any minute and pass out.

Edward motioned and Marguerite, who had been standing silently near the door to the kitchen, began to take away some of the dishes from the table.

Constance began to worry over Elizabeth. She had slumped further down in her chair and she was markedly fatigued. Had the evening been too much? She looked anxiously at Georgina, and with her eyes, directed her to her grandmother. It was time to return the weary matriarch to her bed.

CHAPTER 21

"Hold that torch higher, you deplorable drunk," Edward said to his brother.

The flickering flame was the only light in the large cellar well below Gerard House. They stood in front of a now dusty painting with several rips and tears on the canvas.

Roger could hardly hold the torch straight, but he stared in surprise at the painting. "What a beautiful wench. Who the devil is she and what are we doing down here when I could be drinking some sherry?"

Edward's face softened as he stared at the painting of a woman who could have been a twin to Georgina.

"I commissioned this portrait to impress her," Edward said, speaking to the painting and ignoring Roger. "It wasn't supposed to turn out the way it did."

Roger, losing his patience, grabbed his brother's arm. "Hear now, would you care to tell me what this is all about before I start thinking you've lost your mind for good?"

Edward nodded. "Very well. This stunning woman is Bethany Smythe."

"Dear God, Mother was right. George Kane bears a striking resemblance—" He paused. "But, say again, just why did you have this painting done?" Once he had asked the question, realization swept over his face and a knowing grin emerged, erasing his bewilderment. He slapped Edward hard on the back. "Ahh, Edward, you surprise me! You were bedding this wench, right? And under the same roof as Catherine? You are bolder than I ever imagined. I do believe I will have to reassess my admiration of you and my previous lack of appreciation for your—" He paused to consider his next word. "—accomplishments."

Edward suddenly turned on his brother, rage on his face. "You fool! I had issue with this woman. I had to make sure no one ever knew, and that the illegitimate child never lived to ruin my chance at the Gerard treasure. They both had to disappear!" He stared at his brother, the reflection of the torch flames in his wild eyes. "Do you understand?" He grabbed Roger's shoulders.

Roger stood speechless, staring at his brother until a smirk twisted at his lips. "Oh, but I do understand. I also understand that you now owe me reparation for my continued silence if you want me to keep your murdering ways concealed."

His robust laughter echoed in the dark, expansive cellar. "We will burn in Hell together, dear brother. We shall discuss my funding requirements another day, but there is now another important matter to reflect upon—How do you explain George Kane's uncanny resemblance to your dead consort?"

Edward said, "It could be nothing more than a coincidental resemblance of one person to another, or—" He paused, then grabbed the torch from Roger's hand. "Follow me. We must go grave digging."

179

Edward said, "There will be snow before morning. We must do this tonight." Roger followed closely behind him in the darkness of night. A light snow already covered the cold ground.

They reached the small Gerard cemetery behind the crumbling wall, the gravestones standing like dark ghostly figures in the deepening night. Edward handed a shovel to Roger and took the lantern for himself.

"I am quite frozen," Roger complained. "Why didn't you let me get a warmer coat? This wind is cutting me like a knife."

"You will warm up soon enough, once you put your back behind the shovel."

Swirls of snow whipped and licked their feet. By the time they found the gravestone they sought, the wind shrieked wildly, sounding like a howling banshee. It blew so hard it actually snuffed out the lantern Edward held.

Roger continued to whine. "Why must this be done on a night like this?"

"Because, foolish brother, our inheritance could be in danger if there is not a body in this grave. Now dig, dig for all you're worth, for you may not have much worth at all!"

Roger shivered and began clearing the snow off the mound. He read the inscription on the small gravestone: Georgina Bethany Gerard. He gasped and looked at Edward.

"This is your baby! A baby girl."

"Yes, fool, now keep digging."

When Roger finished with removing most of the snow, he began thrusting the shovel into the frozen ground itself. "I will be at this the whole night," he complained, pausing to catch his breath.

Edward pointed down at the mound. "You keep digging. I will go back to the gardening shed and fetch a pick." He set off, leaving Roger alone.

Roger was regretting getting wound up with his brother's past crimes, even though Edward had certainly handed him the perfect opportunity to guarantee a split of whatever treasure there was to be had in the Will. He went back to digging with redoubled effort. So intently did he continue with his task, that he took no notice of the snow that had begun to fall. It had arrived earlier than expected.

"I've got the pick," Edward called, coming up to him. "And I found a coat for you in the shed."

Roger put the coat on and continued to work with the pick until he had broken through the frozen earth and reached the softer soil beneath it. He switched back to the shovel and was then somewhat surprised when it finally struck something hard. He stopped and called out, "Edward!"

Edward peered over the yawning hole. "It should be small—can you hand it up to me?"

Roger cleared off the soft earth from the top of the small, black oblong box. He had no intention of touching or lifting it up to Edward. "Just pass down the lantern," he shouted against the growing wind. Edward had managed to fire up the lantern again.

"Damn you, I cannot get it to remain lit in this wind!" Edward growled. "I must see what is inside."

"Then keep relighting it while I remove the lid!" Roger yelled back. Edward attempted to cradle the lantern to keep it away from the wind.

Roger set the shovel against the dirt wall and pulled the lid up.

"Hurry!" Edward yelled.

"It is stuck," Roger replied, looking up at his brother.

"Use the pick and pry it open."

Roger hesitated. It was such a tiny coffin.

"Hurry, now is not the time to falter."

Roger lifted the pick and, using the beveled side as a wedge, sprung the top free. He tossed the cover aside in one, swift motion. Edward held the fluttering lantern over the hole in the ground.

Inside, was a small body wrapped in sheets of muslin.

"Your daughter is here," Roger said, "Can we go home now?"

"Unwrap the body," Edward screamed. "Hurry. I must be sure."

"I will not. I will not desecrate a body."

In one swift move, Edward threw himself into the gaping hole in the ground. He began to peel away the layers of wrapped muslin, feeling a hard, lumpy form beneath the fabric. Roger gasped with relief when his brother found only lumps of grey rocks were inside all the wrapping. Edward stared silently, still holding some of the muslin in one hand.

"I have been betrayed," Edward finally said in shock. "Grayson double crossed me."

"Grayson?" Roger asked. "You mean that old grey and withered handyman that shows up occasionally at Gerard House—" Roger suddenly stopped talking, his eyes opening wide in amazement. "Dear God! Georgina is your daughter's name and George Kane is Georg—"

"Do not prattle on. If Georgina is indeed alive, I stand to lose everything I have worked for and I will not allow that to happen."

"But, but—" Roger stammered. "But if George Kane is indeed your daughter Georgina, then Constance—"

"Maybe that is why the wench wanted no part of you. And that's also why she may know more than we even imagine." Edward looked for a way out of the grave.

"What utter debauchery!" Roger said in a loud voice. "A disgusting scandal right under our noses! What choices do we have?"

"Accidents happen in so many ways," Edward said with a wicked grin. "This time, I won't leave the job to some idiot peasant."

Edward stepped up on the coffin after putting the lid back on and climbed his way back up to the top. He reached out a hand for Roger. "If I didn't need you, I would leave you right in that hole and cover up your screams with all this dirt."

Roger scrambled up, a scowl on his face. He dusted off the dirt from the old coat. "You are not getting rid of me that easily."

Edward pointed a finger at his brother. "And I warn you now, that bitch—Miss Beechum—will meet her end as well. I missed with a malfunctioning pistol once, but what I now have in mind for her will not miss."

"Must she die?"

Edward was appalled. "You fool! You still hope to bed her?"

Roger did not answer.

"Your silence is admission enough," Edward said, shaking his head. "We do not know what the wench knows. No woman is worth losing a fortune over."

Roger bowed his head. "Then do what you must. I will comfort myself with the thoughts of all the whores I will be able to buy in London." He grinned with sudden, unbridled anticipation, even in the wind and snow.

Edward saw the change in his brother. "Good! Now cover up that worthless grave and meet me back at the house. I must find out who George Kane really is."

Constance stepped out of Elizabeth's room and gently closed the door behind her. She did not want to wake her. She hadn't moved but a few feet when she became aware of someone behind her. It was Edward.

"Elizabeth is asleep," she told him. "She had a very exhausting night."

"Miss Beechum, I am not here to see my mother," Edward said. "I was hoping to have the opportunity to speak with you about a delicate matter."

Constance nodded. She couldn't help but notice that he appeared disheveled, and there were clumps of dirt and snow on his boots and pantaloons.

"First," he said, "I want to express my apologies about my rude behavior during dinner tonight. My mother sometimes brings out the worst in me." He offered a tight smile while his eyes moved over her in such a manner that it made Constance feel naked. She wanted to cross her arms over her chest to prevent his gawking eyes from settling on her too exposed breasts.

"I know," he went on, "that I have not given you much evidence of appreciation since you have been here, but my grief over mother's impending death—and the obvious stress— have conspired to make me quite inaccessible."

"I understand," she said. What else could she say? She was tired and wanted nothing more than to get to her room and bed.

He smiled again. "I knew you would understand. That is why I am taking the liberty of asking a favor of you. I feel I was especially rude to Mr. Kane, and I would very much like to see him in private to issue a personal apology. I have a book I would like to show him regarding naval navigation that he might find useful for his novel. I will need to go to my personal library for the book, and if you would be so kind to ask Mr. Kane to stay a bit longer so that we may talk, I would be very appreciative."

Constance couldn't help but wonder what Edward really wanted with George Kane. But she was equally curious and could not refuse his request.

"I would be happy to advise him of your request as soon as I go back downstairs."

His smile widened. "You have no idea how much I appreciate your service and your kindness." He reached out and put a hand on her arm.

His touch was ice cold and it set a prickly fear racing down her back. She drew away and told him that she should be on her way so as not to keep Mr. Kane waiting long.

"By all means," he said as she walked away. "Do hurry."

CHAPTER 22

Edward never showed up and once it got too late, Georgina offered her good night to Constance and Catherine who were still keeping him company in the sitting room. She wanted nothing more than to pick Constance up and carry her off to her cottage where they would make passionate love; but there were more important things to attend to this night.

She pressed her lips on Constance's hand, and then Catherine's hand, and made her way home. By the time she got to the cottage, twilight had long since given way to complete darkness. The wind roared as it came off the sea, and overhead the moon and stars were blotted out by a blanket of low-floating clouds.

She could not forget the sight of Constance and the beautiful dress that revealed so much of her. But she had business to do on this cold, blustery night.

Somewhere out there, she knew British war ships were gliding across the coast, laying in wait for American frigates and sloops, like circling sharks. And the American small ships, Essex and Wasp, were also out there like sitting prey. She had to get her charts and lantern ready, pack up her telescope, and head to the top of the crumbling lighthouse at the pinnacle of Lighthouse Pointe. Each night she undertook the signals could be her last. If she stumbled on the broken, jagged stone steps that still led to the top of the lighthouse, she could fall and break her neck. If she was spotted by any of the British ships, they could fire off a round or maneuver close enough to take a shot from the bridge of the vessel. Worse yet, they could land in the cove and swarm the Pointe with redcoats.

She entered the cottage and immediately noticed that her privacy had been invaded once again. Someone had been inside her home, and this time they had turned every drawer inside out. Her belongings spilled out on the floor. Muddy footprints led into her sleeping room. On closer inspection, she realized there was more than one set of footprints.

She made a quick check of the maps and charts and breathed a sigh of relief. Every item she required was still there. She ran to her bedroom and found every piece of clothing she owned strewn over her bed, the chair, and covering the floor. The drawers to her dresser were sitting open, her unmentionables tossed about. She panicked when she noticed the few items of femininity that she allowed herself to indulge in.

She reached down to pick up the small, lace-trimmed satin pillows filled with perfumed powder that had been tossed on the floor. And her frilly underwear was left hanging over her oval mirror. Georgina's heart began to race like a galloping horse that had traveled miles without resting. Something unforeseen was amiss, because this certainly was not a robbery. Why had they taken nothing? She fought hard to control her rage, but fear began to trickle through her insides.

There was no time to clean everything up. She sighed wearily and walked back out to the main living room and the fireplace. She rubbed her frozen hands and watched the flames dance before her eyes. Her thoughts returned to

187

Constance. In all her years of solitude and working for the American government, she had not met many women.

I wish to God I had met Constance under different circumstances. I have fallen in love with a woman for the first time in my life, and the poor lady is in that miserable house and in danger because of me.

Georgina slammed her fist down hard on the mantle. With renewed determination, she grabbed the lantern, telescope, maps and charts. She stopped a moment on the porch and looked toward Gerard mansion. She ached to be inside, with Constance.

She worked her way carefully up the steps to the very top of the lighthouse and looked toward the mouth of the cove. There was no sign of either the Essex or the Wasp. For almost an hour, Georgina paced back and forth, using her telescope to search for British ships and the American sloops. Suddenly, she spotted the murky shapes of two small ships. They were flying the American flag.

She began to signal with her lamp. From one of the ships she decrypted the word: Icestone

Georgina answered: Terra

The other ship then signaled that they were sailing into the cove. She would meet them and hand over the map with the positions of the British ships that had been passed down to her. If the coordinates were correct, the Essex and the Wasp could sail past the British and avoid being boarded, thus saving American sailors from being captured, tortured, and pressed into service for His Majesty, the King of England.

Constance was relieved to finally get out of her evening dress, wash and refresh herself, and fall exhausted into her bed. Her thoughts went from Georgina to the strange behavior of both Edward and Roger. Why had Edward asked her to

delay Georgina at Gerard House for a private meeting and then disappeared without showing up? Where did he go? When questioned about his absence, Catherine was also bewildered. What did Edward really have in mind for George Kane? And where was Roger?

She was too tired and did not wish to struggle against the sleep that overcame her as soon as her head hit the pillow. She had just dozed off when she heard footsteps shuffling in her room. Just as she opened her eyes, she saw a horrifying figure in a black, hooded robe rushing toward her with a pillow held high in the air.

"Die, bitch!" A rough male voice screamed as he threw his body upon her and smothered her face with a foul smelling pillow. His strong body straddled her, pinning her arms against her side. She could move her legs and tried, without avail, to kick back at the man.

"You will not escape me this time, whore!"

Constance could not breathe and the strength of the man was overpowering. The pillow was pushing hard against her face, smashing down on her nose and lips. She thought it was surely the end of her. She would suffocate and no one would find her until tomorrow.

She suddenly heard loud banging on her door.

"Constance! Open the door!" It sounded like Georgina.

Immediately, the hooded figure released her, leaving the pillow over her head. Constance flung the pillow to the floor and sat up in bed in time to see her attacker sneak away behind a secret panel at the fireplace.

Georgina banged on the door again. "Constance, are you there?" Her voice was urgent.

Constance was still gasping for breath as she made her way to the door, undid the bolt, and opened the door. She flung herself into Georgina's arms. "I am sorry," she sobbed. "I cannot stop the tears."

"I'm here, my love," Georgina said gently. "I will not allow any harm to come to you."

"Georgina—" Constance tried to calm her uneven breathing. "I know what I am about to tell you may sound unbelievable, but—" She inhaled deeply and exhaled slowly, several times, to calm her racing heart, with Georgina tightly holding her hand. "Edward—your father—just tried to kill me." She began weeping again. She pointed to the fireplace. "There is a hidden entrance... Go look, I'm sure you will find it. He frightened me once before, shortly after I arrived here. He appeared out of nowhere, and I distinctly remembered not hearing my door open. Now I know why."

Georgina studied her face closely. "That is a serious charge, my darling."

"And I do not make these charges lightly," Constance said. "Please hear me out." Constance explained to Georgina about seeing Edward in his hooded black robe, and how he'd nonchalantly walked past her in the candle-lit hallway one night. "I actually saw him and several others—all dressed in the same attire—on the road when I came here to Gerard House."

Georgina led her to the bed and then went to check out the wall behind the fireplace. She could not believe her eyes. There was indeed a stone door there. She was about to shove it open when Marguerite ran into the room, dressed in a flannel shift, her hands flailing.

"Oh, you must come, Miss Constance and Mr. Kane! It's Mistress Elizabeth—she's in a bad state." Her voice became shrill as she became more panicked.

190

CHAPTER 23

Constance hardly had time to dwell on what had happened to her. When she, Georgina and Marguerite arrived in Elizabeth's room, she was writhing in pain. Her eyes were staring into space and glazed. She did not seem to recognize them—even Georgina.

"I wish to die," she said with a weak voice. "Why will you not allow me to die?"

Constance quickly went for the laudanum. She looked at Georgina, who seemed to be lost in a daze. "Help me give it to her," she said.

"I was afraid tonight was going to be too much for her," Georgina said, looking worriedly at her grandmother. "How long before the drug takes effect?"

"Shortly," Constance said, as she forced a bit of water into Elizabeth's slack mouth. She motioned to Marguerite. "Why don't you light some candles and put another log on the fire?"

Marguerite was slow to move, but she did as she was told, talking as she worked. "The Mistress asked me to stay the night to help clean the kitchen in the morn. She was fine when I left her, Miss."

"No one is blaming you for anything, Marguerite," Georgina assured her.

Elizabeth suddenly shuddered. She opened her eyes and moved her lips but no sound came out. She attempted to lift her hand but could not.

Georgina stared at her grandmother intensely. "I think she has had a stroke," she said, reaching for her hand.

Elizabeth's eyes turned to Constance. She struggled to speak. Spittle ran down the corners of her trembling mouth, but she managed a weak smile. She summoned all her strength and said in a whisper, "Take...care...of her..." Her eyes fluttered and closed. She uttered one great sigh and her head flopped to one side.

Georgina squeezed her hand hard. "Grandmother! Grandmother!"

Constance put her hand on her shoulder. "She is gone, Georgina."

She eased her hand free of her grandmother's hold, and shook her head. "It was all so quick. I—" She turned away from Constance.

Marguerite, standing quiet behind them, began to cry. The door suddenly swung open. Edward stood looking angrily into the room.

"Your mother has just passed," Constance said, wiping the tears from her eyes.

Edward said nothing. He entered the room and looked at the body of his mother, then cast a scowl at Georgina.

"What are you doing here?" There was venom in his voice.

Constance took hold of Georgina's hand. "I am fortunate that Mr. Kane stayed." She cast a defiant gaze at him, although her insides were turning to pudding. He had tried to kill her only moments ago.

He seemed to gather his emotions and looked directly at her. "Well, Miss Beechum, you realize that your services are no longer needed here."

"Yes."

"I will see that you have transportation back to your home."

"If I might stay for Elizabeth's interment—"

"There will be no need for that," he replied tersely. "Burial arrangements will be private."

"Surely," Georgina said, "Miss Beechum means that—"

"I have no wish to discuss the matter with either of you. As for you—" His face contorted in a wicked scowl "Mr. Kane, since my mother is now gone and I am Master of Gerard House, any contract you had with her during your stay in the cottage is hereby rescinded. You can begin to move your things out in the morning."

He puffed out his chest and quickly walked out of the room. Georgina, her face filled with rage, took off after him. Constance put out a hand and held her back.

"Let him go, Darling. He does not realize the surprise that awaits him when her Last Will and Testament is read." She smiled. "It is a far better punishment than violence."

Georgina looked back at Marguerite, who still stood pressed up against the corner wall with her mouth agape.

"But the bastard tried to kill you, my love, she whispered. "I will not let him get away with that."

Constance wanted to kiss and calm her lover, but there was the matter of Marguerite in the room. She called the maid over to her.

"Marguerite, I know this is all rather much to understand, but I must ask you to please go back to your room and forget everything you've heard tonight. May I trust you to keep it all a secret? Elizabeth wanted it this way."

Marguerite's eyes darted from the corpse on the bed to Constance. "But Mistress Elizabeth...who will look after—"

"I will take care of everything," Constance assured her. "Now, please, try and get some rest, and I would ask that you stay on tomorrow as well."

The bewildered maid merely nodded her head and slowly backed out of the room, closing the door behind her.

"Can we trust her?" Georgina asked.

193

Constance walked up to her and wrapped her arms around Georgina. She could no longer control her desire to kiss and comfort her lover. She kissed her gently and rubbed her shoulders.

"Marguerite has been somewhat of an ally. I trust her. Darling, what we need now is to set up more candles for your grandmother for the night vigil until the morn, and until word is sent for the mortician and the constable in Castine. We shall also need to send a post to my Uncle Merriweather. He is the executor of your grandmother's estate and Will."

Georgina leaned down and kissed her lightly. "Very well. I shall go downstairs for the candles and candleholders first." She opened the door. "Tomorrow, I shall ride to Castine and post the notice to your uncle."

Constance took hold of her arm. "And prepare for the truth and the ugliness your grandmother's passing will bring to the family."

Georgina smiled sadly. "I've been preparing a long time for this day, but with you by my side, it will be far easier to face." She walked out the door.

It took Georgina longer than she wanted to gather candlesticks and candles from the sitting parlor and dining hall. She didn't feel comfortable leaving Constance alone. With her grandmother gone, Edward or Roger was capable of anything.

When she felt she had gathered up enough, she practically bounded up the steps to the balcony hallway and over to Elizabeth's room. She was thankful she had seen nothing of Edward or Roger, or even Catherine. Surely, Edward had already spread the news of his mother's passing.

As she entered Elizabeth's room, she found it empty. The three candles Constance had arranged surrounding Elizabeth's bed burned brightly. But Constance was not there.

Her heart was beating so hard, she felt sure it would burst forth from her chest. Something was wrong. She left the room and looked down the length of the hall, calling Constance's name. When there was no response, Georgina took off, heading back toward the balcony.

As she rounded the corner, she stopped in her tracks. Roger was blocking the way. He was disheveled and held a saber in his right hand. In the light of the candles, his eyes glowed wildly.

"So, my dear little niece...it is so nice to meet you finally." He grinned menacingly. "Yes, your father—" He paused and cocked his head. "My, that does sound odd. Well, your father and I took the liberty of visiting you at the cottage, and since you were not home, we decided to make ourselves at home. Oh, and what we found—" He shook his head. "How disgusting and perverted you are, little niece." He nearly spat the words out. "And you took advantage of Constance in your perversions."

"You had no right!" Georgina hissed, her anger mounting.

"You are much bolder now than when you were George Kane."

"Where is Constance?" Georgina demanded.

"You still see her as a prize? Is there no end to your repugnant charade?"

"Get out of my way, Uncle!" Georgina started forward.

"Hold it right there." Roger thrust his saber out. "There is no Constance here to plead for you not accept my challenge."

"You are too drunk. I will not fight you in your present state. Now let me pass."

"I have had wine, true enough, but not so much to stop me from killing you, little niece. You are nothing but a stranger to me, truth be told."

Georgina stared him down. "I ask again. Where is Constance? I demand to know."

Roger's eyes fixed upon hers. "Of course, it is the lovely wench you came for—I forgot." He burst into laughter. "And I never thought Edward was that interested in her for his own purposes, but that just goes to prove that you can never really know what another man is truly about. Not even your own brother."

"What are you prattling about, man?" Georgina was losing her patience and time was running out. She had to find Constance. With her secret out, her father was infinitely more dangerous. She had to find her before something unspeakable happened.

"Edward has her," Roger said casually.

Georgina started forward in a rage, but the point of Roger's saber stabbed lightly against her chest.

"We will fight like men, since that is how you choose to live." The grin on his face was without mirth.

"You fool!" Georgina shouted.

"Draw!"

Georgina uttered a curse as she drew her saber swiftly. She did not wish to harm her uncle. She'd been trained by some of the best sailors in the United States Navy. She could outdo him in minutes.

"This is not a fight that I choose, Uncle. I do not wish to do you harm."

Roger attacked wildly without warning. Georgina parried each clumsy lunge without stress.

"I will kill you!" Roger screamed.

Georgina took a cut from his saber on her left shoulder. Roger laughed out loud.

"I could easily have finished you off, but, my little mouse, I'd much rather play the cat a little longer."

Georgina was hoping to slash him across the wrist and force him to drop his weapon, but she soon realized that her uncle's words were not the meaningless bravado of a drunkard. He fully intended to kill her, his niece. She had no choice but to defend herself and fight as if her life depended on it. She instantly changed from purely defensive tactics to aggressively ruthless, life or death swordplay.

196

Roger fell back from her onslaught. "You are far better than I suspected," he said, breathless.

"Then I suggest, nay, plead, that you put your sword down and save your life," Georgina said. "Help me find Constance instead."

"And what of my honor, negligible as it may be?"

Georgina hardened her gaze. "You will have no worries for your honor if you are a corpse." Georgina rushed him with such a fury, that Roger cringed, backed off and tripped over his own foot. He fell to the ground, dropping the saber. Georgina towered over him, sword pointed at his chest.

"Kill me," Roger shouted. "Go ahead, run me through."

"I ask again. Where is Constance?"

"She belongs to Edward now and whatever use he intends for her."

"Tell me where he has her!" Georgina screamed.

Roger only shrugged.

"I have wasted enough time with you, Uncle." Georgina turned her back on him. She walked only a few yards down the hall when from behind her, Roger gave a hideous shriek. She whirled around quickly. In the dim candlelight, she hurled her saber like a spear at Roger's rushing form.

Roger's body seemed to be lifted off the floor and then crumpled like an unstrung marionette. Georgina's sword was buried deep in her uncle's chest. She could not find a tear to shed for a man who had wanted to kill her first.

"You would have it no other way," she said as she pulled her sword loose, blood still dripping, and continued her search for Constance. She had to remain focused. Constance was all that mattered.

CHAPTER 24

Moments before Georgina entered Elizabeth's room, Edward had snuck up behind Constance and covered her face with a handkerchief drenched in laudanum. She struggled only minutes before passing out in his arms.

"Come, come," he whispered in her ear. "You should not be so frightened. Soon, you will be aware of everything." He uttered a low laugh as he swept her lifeless body over his left shoulder. Before walking out of the room, he went to his mother's corpse on the bed. There was a gleam of madness in his eyes.

"You are dead. You are finally dead." He moved closer to the bed. "You took too long and kept many secrets from me. I thought you would be more considerate of your son. I will not allow my bastard daughter to take any part of the treasure that belongs to me. I will kill her first."

With Constance still unconscious, he worked his way slowly to his room and carefully opened the secret door that led to the secret tunnels deep beneath Gerard House.

Finally, he carried her into a small, musty room where there was little but old pieces of furniture. Edward dropped her into a dusty chair.

By now, Constance had come to. She wiped her eyes groggily and searched her surroundings. Edward stood before her.

"Do not bother to scream. No one will hear you down here. We are well below the foundations of the house—solid rock and earth. These tunnels and secret rooms were the Gerard's way of helping the British during the war. It was the least we could do." He chuckled wickedly.

Constance was afraid, but defiant and confident that Georgina would find her. "What do you want with me?" She asked. "I am not without strength."

Edward cackled and it echoed through the room. "It will do you no good to expend your energies down here."

She stood up and started toward him. "I shall be free."

He came at her, pushing her hard with enormous strength. She fought back and slapped his face with all her might.

"You bitch!" he screamed. "You will pay a heavy price for that!"

Constance attempted to rush past him, but he grabbed her by the wrist and twisted until she was in so much pain that she fell upon her knees.

"You are now in the proper position before me."

"You are mad!" Constance screamed, grimacing in pain.

"No, not mad!" Edward shouted. "I assure you I am quite sane. My followers and I merely see the world for what it truly is. Soon, you shall be part of our world!"

"Please, Mr. Gerard!" she cried. "Let me go. What use have you for me?"

He leaned forward, coming so close that she could smell his breath. "A better use for you than you could ever imagine for yourself," he said. But that answer must wait for later. Now, I must leave to see if my inept brother has dispatched of a little pest that I thought had been eradicated twenty three years ago."

"You are a monster to want your own daughter dead," Constance said. "Elizabeth was right."

"My mother is now dead," he said. "No one is going to stand in the way of what is mine."

"You are not only a monster, but a disgusting and greedy toad of a man as well."

"Call me what you like," he sneered, "but before this night is done, you will be my bride in darkness."

"Your what?" Constance cried out.

Edward cackled again. "Oh, it will be a very special ceremony," he said with relish. "And my dear Catherine will be your Maid of Honor." He laughed manically. "Tonight, you will understand who and what I truly am."

"No!" Constance screamed. "Please, release me and I will go away!"

He grabbed her roughly and took her back to the chair where he tied her hands behind her back and then secured her feet to the legs of the chair.

"I will return with haste. I've prepared something special for you." He took off to another room. When he came back, he had a goblet with some dark red liquid in it. He put it to her lips.

"Drink it. This will reward you with very pleasant dreams."

Constance refused to drink, moving her head away from the goblet. Angrily, he grabbed her jaw and forced her mouth open, pouring the liquid down her throat.

"You will sleep now," he told her. "I have preparations to make and cannot have you down here awake."

He stood over her and watched as the sleep potion took effect. Constance slumped in the chair, out cold. Unable to restrain himself, Edward reached out and ran his fingers down her face and neck.

"In a short time," he whispered, "You will be consort to the Prince of Darkness himself."

He reluctantly withdrew his hand before reaching her breasts and turned away, making his way back up the stone steps to Gerard House.

Edward called his brother's name throughout the house, finally heading up to the balcony and Elizabeth's room. As he approached the balcony hallway, he saw a form lying on the ground. It was Roger and he was moaning.

"Roger!" he said, as he reached the dying man. "This cannot be you!"

Roger moaned again in pain. "I am dying," he whimpered. "Help me." He reached for his brother's hand. "I am frightened."

"Who did this to you?" Edward asked. He backed away from Roger's outreached hand.

"Georgina."

Edward's howl filled the hall.

"Please," Roger begged.

Edward remained still and silent as he watched his brother die.

He stood a moment staring at the form of his dead brother. "Now there is no one left who knows my secret except Catherine, and she will meet her own accident soon enough. And my bastard daughter will join my brother in hell." There was no one to hear him but Death.

Edward turned to walk away when Georgina appeared in his path.

"Edward!" She yelled. "Where is Constance?"

He smirked, his face appearing ghoulish in the candles' light. "So that is all that matters to you. No love for your dear old father?" He suddenly reached out to the two flickering candles on the wall and quickly snuffed them out, leaving them in darkness.

"You will not have her for your perversions. My misbegotten daughter, you will not live long enough to enjoy your immoral pleasures. I know you killed Roger and if you value your life, you will leave Gerard House, this country, and go far away."

"I will not let you get past me," Georgina said.

Edward inched his way along the hall until he found one of the unlit candleholders. He detached it from the wall and hurled it across the balcony to draw Georgina away from him. She rushed toward the sound, not sure where she was headed. Edward took the chance and ran across the balcony and down the stairs, leaving the sound of his wicked cackling trailing behind him.

Georgina was annoyed with herself for falling for such a simple trick. She felt her way back through the hallway toward her grandmother's room, took a burning candle and re-lit the candles in the balcony hallway. She had wasted too much time and had to continue searching for Constance, but where to look? She decided to go back downstairs.

She had just crossed the foyer when she heard heavy knocking on the front door. She blew out the taper she held and stood aside with her cutlass ready to thrust.

The door opened and two men stepped inside, one wearing a wide carriage hat and carrying an expensive cane. She could hardly see them but thought she recognized one of them.

"Hello?" the taller, heftier stranger called. "Is there anyone here at all?"

Georgina leaped between him and the door, taking the chance that neither of them carried firearms. She placed the point of the cutlass against the broad of the man's chest. "Shut the door and tell me who the devil you are."

One of the men did as she asked and closed the door.

"What is all this about?" asked the taller man. "It is I who should ask who you are."

The shorter man shuffled forward and Georgina saw that it was Grayson. "What is going on here, Grayson?" She still kept the point of her weapon nudging the other man. She cast her gaze at him.

"Declare yourself, Sir."

"Elizabeth will know who I am, and I was hoping my niece would greet my arrival instead of a sword. I am William Merriweather, barrister and executor of the Gerard estate."

Georgina lowered her sword and sheathed it. "Why did you not say so?"

"You scarcely gave me the chance with a saber near my throat. And now I am demanding to know who you are."

"I'm sorry, Mr. Merriweather. I hope you will forgive me. I am Georgina Gerard, Elizabeth's granddaughter."

She heard Grayson clear his throat but he said nothing.

"Now will you care to tell me what in heaven's name is going on here? And why are you dressed like that?"

"My grandmother has passed just this night," Georgina said.

"You have my sympathies. I had hoped to see her before the end," Merriweather said. "I've been her confidante and barrister for over forty years."

"She went very peacefully. I was able to be there when she passed, as was Constance. And my dress, Sir, is my personal business."

William Merriweather frowned and peered around at his surroundings. "And where is my niece? I trust she has been providing proper care and services."

"We should proceed into the parlor. There is better light and I can explain what I know."

All three worked their way to the sitting parlor, where candles still blazed bright and the fire in the fireplace was barely still alive.

Merriweather removed his hat and Georgina noted he was a healthy looking man of about fifty or so, with grey streaks splashed at his temples.

"Edward has lost his wits and has kidnapped your niece. We must find her immediately. I fear for her life."

"I was beginning to doubt my wisdom of sending my niece here. Explain what you are talking about, and do it quickly."

Georgina related everything Roger had told her.

"And Roger?" Merriweather asked. "What of him?"

"Dead, I suppose by now." She explained what happened with their duel.

"Good God, what happened here?" Merriweather's eyes were wide with shock.

"Exactly what I have told you," Georgina said. "I cannot even guess why Edward has kidnapped Constance. I only know that she is in great danger. He has gone mad."

"We should search the house, Mr. Merriweather and Miss Georgina." Grayson spoke for the first time. "We should start with every room in the occupied wing."

"It's as good a plan as any," Georgina said, concern burning in her worried eyes. "Let us get started."

They found nothing in any of the rooms on the downstairs floor. Even Edward's room gave them no clue. The second floor search proved to be just as futile. Not even Catherine was to be found.

"Constance's room is the last to search," Georgina said impatiently.

Merriweather was surprised that his niece's room was not in the same wing as the other living quarters. He looked at Georgina. "Was there a reason for her lodging here that you are aware of?"

"I have a bad feeling about that, Mr. Merriweather." She remembered the secret door behind the fireplace and suspected Edward had his own perverse reasons for putting Constance in that particular room.

They stepped inside the room and Georgina headed for the fireplace.

"Do you hear that?" Merriweather asked.

"Yes," Georgina said as she neared the wall behind the fireplace. "It sounds like some sort of chanting."

Georgina motioned for the two men to follow her behind the wall of the fireplace. She put her ear to the secret door and listened. "It sounds like a Mass," she whispered. "We must open this door. I believe it is a secret passage and it could lead us to where he is holding your niece."

All three began to pound on the door. "No use," Merriweather said. It must be locked from the other side."

Georgina handed her taper to Grayson, went over and picked up one of the chairs in the room, and then used it as a battering ram. The legs of the chair shattered against the strong stone door. "It's no use. We need strong axes and crowbars," she said. She tossed the chair on the floor and walked to the window. "I have but one last resort to get to Constance. I must try."

She looked out and saw the spars of the Essex where she lay at anchor in Lighthouse Pointe cove, waiting for Georgina. She had nearly forgotten about the ship. In her agony and search for Constance, she was putting one of the nation's ships in dire jeopardy. And yes, the Essex could be her only hope for saving Constance. She turned abruptly to Merriweather. "I will bring the tools we need. It will take me some time, but I will return. Do not leave this room."

"Where are you going?" asked Merriweather. "Where will you get such tools?"

"I will bring the tools," Georgina repeated. "I shall need to take one of the horses from the stable and return as quickly as possible."

"Good luck, then. God speed!"

"Thank you, kind Sir!" she called as she rushed out of the room.

CHAPTER 25

The soporific effect of the drug Constance had been forced to drink was beginning to wear off and as she regained some of her senses, she realized that she was no longer in the small room, tied to the chair. Though she still lacked the strength to open her eyelids, she could tell from the sounds in the room that she was in a much larger area with several people nearby. There were voices speaking in whispers so she could not make out what they were saying.

Very slowly she forced her eyes open and looked up to a vaulted ceiling of stones. There were several torches burning that cast a flickering light throughout the cavernous room. Her heart skipped when she realized she was surrounded by several cowled figures.

"She is awake," a man's voice said. "I will tell the Master."

Constance sat up, and as she moved, she saw that she had been wrapped in layers of sheer, black gauze-like material. Underneath, she was naked. She wanted to scream and ask where she was and what was happening, but she was still weak and confused.

"The wench is a good looker," the third man exclaimed.

She tried to stand, but her legs felt like string and she could not support her weight.

"The Master bids you bring his bride," a man said.

The two hooded men approached and lifted her from the couch she'd been laying on. She was carried into another huge room where the light from a multitude of burning torches glowed against the walls. Directly ahead, behind an altar like none she'd ever seen before, stood two baleful figures.

The altar was draped in black lace, and a black inverted crucifix sat in the center which was flanked by two candelabras at each end, burning seven black candles. Constance stared at the candles and forced herself to remember where she had seen black candles before. It was Edward! The night when she had witnessed him coming up the stairs at Gerard House, heavy with drink or something else that put him in a trance, he had carried such candles. She tried to scream, but found that she could not even manage a whimper.

She was carried before the black robed man standing behind the altar. His face was covered by a black half mask of fur and on his head he wore two large, black goat horns. He was imposing and frightening and Constance tried desperately to get free.

He bowed before her and then stepped back as her two captors sat her atop the altar.

"This night," one of the men said, "we will celebrate the mighty power of our Master's virility."

The others in the room intoned their approval.

Constance's head began to clear and she became even more aware of her surroundings. It was quite clear what this room was. It was a chapel, but a chapel to Lucifer, the devil. Underneath the torches on the wall, sat tripods that held copper bowls. They issued flames of different colors. The sickening sweet scent of perfumes permeated the air.

"To make our pleasure even greater," one of the hooded men echoed, "we will drink the wine of love and blood."

Another man handed him a large goblet and a dove which lay still, barely moving. The man pulled a dagger from his robe and without hesitation slit the throat of the dove, making sure that each drop fell into the goblet. He flung the dead dove to the ground, lifted the goblet to the goat-headed leader, and then brought it to Constance.

"Drink," he ordered. "Drink!"

She did not have enough strength to fight him. The cup was forced to her lips and the warm blood trickled down her throat. She wanted to throw it back up.

The group of three hooded men shouted their approval.

Once Constance stopped her gagging, the man turned to the horned figure in black and raised his hands. "Let the night of pleasure begin!"

The other hooded figure that had stood silent behind the altar now stepped before the altar and let the robe fall to the floor.

Constance gasped. It was Catherine, standing naked for all in the room to see! One of the other robed men pulled his robe off and came forward to join her, also naked. Constance did not recognize the man. He began to run his hands over every part of Catherine's shapely body. They both embraced and began to writhe and moan.

Constance wanted to look away as the couple dropped to the floor and laid in each other's arms. Another of the cowled men approached her.

"It is your time to be the living altar of our sacrifice to the Prince of Darkness!" He forced her to lie back on the altar.

Finally, the leader with goat horns and mask spoke. "Behold!" he shouted. "My bride—and the bride to all of you, after I am done with her." He began an incantation Constance did not understand, but she thought she recognized the voice. Fear gnawed at her insides.

The leader approached the altar and stared down at her. He leaned down close and whispered. "A better use for you than you could ever have imagined for yourself."

Constance reached up and uncovered his face. It was Edward!

I will not let him have me. Never! She summoned all her strength and in one huge effort, opened her mouth and screamed louder than she had ever screamed in her life.

"Very well, gentlemen, let us have at this door." Running like a madwoman, Georgina had returned with picks, crowbars, and two pistols for extra protection. "I could find no ax, but these picks will do."

"Where did you get all of this?" Merriweather asked, admiring one of the guns.

"It is a long story—one that I shall gladly share with you when we get Constance to safety."

All three took to attacking the stone door with the large picks. It didn't take long for Georgina to be able to jam a crowbar inside an opening they had created. She lent her weight to the crowbar and it began to pull back the stone door.

"Quick!" She urged the two men through the gap.

Once they got on the other side, they unbolted the door and Georgina followed them through.

They stood at the top of the long, narrow stairs.

"Do not use the firearms unless I order you to do so, or if it becomes a matter of life and death," she said. Captain Newman of the Essex had loaned her the pistols under the condition they came back fully loaded, if at all possible.

They lit three torches and followed the narrow staircase down and through the tunnel until they came to a point that radiated out to several other passageways.

Georgina gestured for them to stop as they listened to the sound of chanting. The sound was so close, it had to come from just ahead and to their left. "This way," she said, brandishing her cutlass.

The voices became louder. She thought she heard Lucifer's name invoked in an incantation. Georgina paused, trying to push the fear deep down into the pit of her stomach.

Merriweather asked, "What is it, Miss Gerard?"

"Something evil is going on down here, and we will need all our wits to confront it. We must remember that getting Constance to safety is our only concern."

She handed her torch to Grayson and told him to snuff it out. "Wait for me here." She crouched low and proceeded to what appeared to be an entrance to another room. She motioned for the two men to move forward. "When I rush in," she whispered, "you will follow me and make yourselves known to all persons in that room. Point your firearms but do not fire. Only if any of them attempt to stop me will you shoot to kill."

"How do we know how many people are in there, Miss Georgina?" asked Grayson.

"No matter how many, my good man. We cannot change the odds but only make sure we get Constance out of there." Her green eyes burned with determination.

"Now!" Georgina shouted as she rushed into the cavernous chapel.

Constance screamed and Georgina saw that she lay wrapped in black, sprawled atop an altar. The sound of Georgina's voice silenced everyone. She raised her saber in threat as she advanced toward Edward and Constance at the altar.

"Back off, man!"

Edward tried to pull Constance in front of him, but Georgina had already leaped over the altar and blocked his way.

"I will kill you this time!" Edward looked desperately to his followers. "Don't just stand there, fools!" he screamed. "Seize her!"

"No one move," Georgina shouted. "There are firearms trained on all of you."

210

"Anyone who lays a hand on my niece dies here tonight. I don't miss with a pistol!" Merriweather shouted from the cave entrance. Both he and Grayson kept their guns pointed.

"You will not take me alive!" screamed Edward. He held out a large dagger he had pulled from his robe. But even before he could lunge at Georgina, a shot rang out. There was a wisp of smoke from Grayson's pistol.

Edward fell heavy to the floor, the blood already pooling around his body. A cry went up from Edward's followers and they began to back off in confusion.

"Get out, all of you, and never come back here," Georgina shouted, and others began to run through other exits from the chapel, like scampering pests. "If you choose to stay, we shall have to turn you over to the constable and you will most assuredly spend a night in the Castine jail." Georgina's words echoed through the room as the final hooded figure disappeared from view.

She waited until the unholy chapel was empty before she turned her attention to Constance. She still lay on the altar, dazed and too frightened to even move. Georgina kissed her and held her tightly.

"My darling, you will be all right," she whispered.

Constance found her voice. "Edward, he was going to—"

"But he did not touch you, Constance," Georgina said.

Merriweather came running toward them. "Is my niece well?"

"Uncle Merriweather?" Constance didn't know if she was still delusional or whether her uncle was really there.

"She is shaken," Georgina said, "but well."

"Thank God, but for heaven's sake," Merriweather said, removing his coat, "put something over her." He handed the coat to Georgina who draped it over Constance.

He looked around the room and shook his head. "Whoever would have thought that something like this could take place in our land in these times?"

Grayson came up quietly to stand beside Georgina. He did not look her in the eye. "Beg pardon, Miss Georgina, but that man once asked something unpardonable of me, and I've been cursed with nightmares since. I wasn't going to let him do it to you." He handed her the pistol.

Merriweather slapped him on the back. "You probably saved Miss Gerard's life, my good man. You've done nothing to be sorry for."

"Why don't we get Constance out of here," Georgina said, making sure Constance was strong enough to stand on her own.

"What of this unholy place?" Grayson asked.

"It should be sealed and forgotten," she said with distaste. "We shall take care of it later."

Without a word, they all made their way through the tunnel and back up the stone steps to Constance's room. Merriweather and Grayson both went outside, closing the door behind them. Georgina sat Constance down on the bed and went to the dowel in search of a dress for her to wear.

She studied Constance's face. "You really scared me, my darling. I could not bear the thought of losing you."

Constance was feeling much better, although her entire body felt a little light, much like a feather. Georgina came to her side. She ran her fingers down her lover's cheek. "I worked too hard finding you to give up so easily."

Constance smiled weakly. "I knew you'd come for me."

Georgina helped her get dressed in a light dress with a shawl draped over her shoulders. They met the two men outside the door, where Constance hugged her uncle tightly.

"I thought you were a delusion down there in that horrid place. I am so glad you are really here, but what are you doing here, Uncle? You sent no post advising me of your visit."

"Well, I began to worry a bit and decided I should combine a meeting with poor Elizabeth and a visit to check in on my favorite niece. It was time to go over her Will and other estate papers. Apparently, I arrived too late for Elizabeth, but just in time for you." He laughed.

"Why don't we go downstairs to the main dining room?" Georgina suggested. "There are many things to explain."

CHAPTER 26

Georgina and Constance sat across the long dining room table with papers from Uncle Merriweather's open briefcase spread out before them. One large candelabra and two oil lamps shed an abundance of light on the scene.

Georgina held up one of the documents in her hand. "So you are saying that I own everything? Gerard House, all the land surrounding it, Lighthouse Pointe, and much of Castine belong to me?" She had a crooked smile as she stared at her grandmother's attorney.

"Well, not all of town," Merriweather pointed out. "You see, your grandmother was a very wise and shrewd business woman. Soon after your grandfather took off to sea and never returned, Elizabeth began to give the upstart bankers of Castine a run for their money. With the good relationship she had developed among the townspeople, and even her staff at Gerard House, she made barter loans and also doled out copious amounts of start-up capital to many of the businesses. The contracts and deeds were written in such a manner that Elizabeth was owner of the loans until the borrower decided to either sell or move. She demanded not a penny of payback, unless—" He lifted a finger in the air. "Unless they wanted to become owners—lock, stock and barrel—of their property or land. At that point, they either had to repay the entire loan back to Elizabeth, or begin paying off the loan in installments. Some of them have been doing just that. There is a hefty sum in an account set up secretly just for you. That is where most of the Gerard money is invested and where you'll find the real Gerard treasure."

"So what you are saying, Uncle," Constance said, "is that Georgina, if she wished, could conceivably demand repayment or take control over these—" she paused, "—parcels of land and businesses?"

"I already control them, my dear," Georgina teased.

"She is correct, in a way," Merriweather added. "Georgina is now holder of very attractive farms and businesses in Castine, including the lumber business."

Georgina put the paper down that she was holding and looked at Merriweather. "What if I have no desire to handle these affairs? Will I be forced to do so now that grandmother is gone?"

Merriweather chuckled. "Oh, good heavens, no. Elizabeth only received periodic posts with updates on the properties and the account statements. My firm handled everything for your grandmother and we can continue to do so if you wish. You have much to consider when making decisions, Miss Gerard, including the house itself." He cast an eye at both Georgina and Constance.

Georgina's face grew serious and she looked straight at Constance. "What an incredible gift my grandmother has left me. And I have been blessed with an even greater gift than money or land." She winked at Constance, and then looked back at Merriweather. "You are right, Sir. I do indeed have much to ponder. I offer you the comfort of Gerard House for both yourself and Grayson, if you should wish to stay the night. After my head has cleared, I should have a better understanding of what all these papers mean in the morn."

Merriweather nodded. "Thank you, Miss Gerard, for your hospitality. I shall send Grayson into Castine to take care of

Elizabeth, Roger and Edward with haste. He shall be disturbing the slumber of many a Castine law officer and mortician, I'm afraid." He began to collect the papers on the table into a leather pouch which he passed to Georgina. "Will you be staying on here, since it is your home, now?"

Georgina didn't take long to consider the answer. "No, Constance and I will be returning to my cottage." She looked intently at her. "She needs to get as far from here as possible tonight. Perhaps she might feel differently tomorrow." She paused and waved a hand at Constance. "Of course, it is up to her to make that decision."

Constance hoped she wasn't blushing again. Her uncle would surely notice and wonder where it was coming from. "I very much would like to get away at least for the night." She reached out and grabbed her uncle's arm. "I do hope you don't mind, Uncle. We can spend some time together tomorrow."

He shook his head and smiled. "Bah, why would you want to spend time with such an old man, anyway? But you might consider what your future will be now that you are no longer employed at Gerard House." He looked at her seriously. "I have no other jobs to offer you."

Constance and Georgina stood, wrapped in each other's arms in the main room of the cottage. The fireplace blazed, and the crackle of the burning wood a mesmerizing sound.

"I know your heart is not into all of that responsibility bequeathed to you in your grandmother's Will," Constance whispered.

Georgina's green eyes sparkled in the firelight. "War is coming, my love, and I will serve a very important part in it, I believe."

Constance turned back the slight pang of fear and disappointment and concentrated instead on the heat

216

coursing through her body. She kissed Georgina passionately, running her hands through her raven tresses.

Georgina smiled down at her. "My heart, my life belongs to you, but my service to my country might call me away. There could be trips to the border. I cannot lie and brush away the danger of the work of a spy who is passionate about her country." She looked away from Constance, then back again. "I love you, my darling Constance. You must know that even if I leave, I shall return to your side always." She took hold of Constance's hands, covering them with light kisses. "I will ask if you would make a home with me at Gerard House. You will have free hand at redecorating and doing whatever you wish with it." She crushed her even tighter into her. "Tell me you will be mine."

"Yes!" Constance answered without hesitation. "Oh, dear God, yes!"

Made in the USA
Lexington, KY
19 December 2011